Jim Colby turned to his staff of highly skilled equalizer agents and said, "Find a way in."

Ian Michaels and Lucas Camp wanted to wait, to quietly meet the demands of the hostage takers and then make a move. Jim couldn't wait any longer. "If we don't do something soon, someone will die."

Lucas stood toe-to-toe with Jim. "We're doing all within our power to find a way in to the Colby Agency offices without detection. We will proceed with caution. It's what Victoria would want."

If anyone in this room knew Jim's mother, Victoria…Lucas did.

Jim had been wrong and he wasn't about to pretend otherwise. He looked to Lucas and then to Ian. "We will neutralize this situation before anyone else is hurt or worse," he assured the men who were as much a part of his family as his own mother. "Whatever it takes."

Ian nodded, his dark eyes uncharacteristically bright. "Whatever it takes."

Lucas looked from one man to the next and repeated that mantra. "Whatever it takes."

DEBRA WEBB

COLBY LOCKDOWN

HARLEQUIN®

TORONTO • NEW YORK • LONDON
AMSTERDAM • PARIS • SYDNEY • HAMBURG
STOCKHOLM • ATHENS • TOKYO • MILAN • MADRID
PRAGUE • WARSAW • BUDAPEST • AUCKLAND

Recycling programs
for this product may
not exist in your area.

ISBN-13: 978-0-373-74509-8

COLBY LOCKDOWN

www.eHarlequin.com

Printed in U.S.A.

ABOUT THE AUTHOR

Debra Webb was born in Scottsboro, Alabama, to parents who taught her that anything is possible if you want it bad enough. She began writing at age nine. Eventually, she met and married the man of her dreams, and tried some other occupations, including selling vacuum cleaners, working in a factory, a day-care center, a hospital and a department store. When her husband joined the military, they moved to Berlin, Germany, and Debra became a secretary in the commanding general's office. By 1985 they were back in the States, and finally moved to Tennessee, to a small town where everyone knows everyone else. With the support of her husband and two beautiful daughters, Debra took up writing again. In 1998, her dream of writing for Harlequin Books came true. You can write to Debra with your comments at P.O. Box 64, Huntland, Tennessee 37345, or visit her Web site at www.debrawebb.com to find out exciting news about her next book.

Books by Debra Webb

*Colby Agency
†The Equalizers
††Colby Agency: Elite Reconnaissance Division
**Colby Agency: Under Siege

Dear Reader,

This year marks a special anniversary for the Colby Agency: ten years of breathtaking suspense in Harlequin Intrigue! As a special treat for the many, many loyal readers, the Colby Agency will be presented to you in an unparalleled six-book series, UNDER SIEGE. Here's a peek of what's to come!

Colby Lockdown—The Colby Agency is under siege from an unknown enemy. For the first time in Colby history, the infamous Equalizers and the most trusted investigators of the agency must come together as a team.

Colby Justice—A mock trial will determine the fate of one member of Chicago's seamy streets. One man will act as judge and executioner. The head of the Colby Agency is trapped amid that nightmare. Her investigators and the Equalizers have one chance and only twenty-four hours to salvage the situation…

Colby Control and *Colby Velocity*—These two back-to-back installments follow the edge-of-your-seat challenges of the cases facing the Colby Agency while Jim Colby and his Equalizers merge into day-to-day operations.

Colby Holiday and *Colby New Year*—As the UNDER SIEGE series comes to a close, the shake-up at the Colby Agency has settled. The Equalizers have meshed fully with the Colby Agency. The dangerous cases to come will require the expert skills and uncanny instincts of this newly formed staff.

So read on! You'll find the Colby Agency only at Harlequin Intrigue. For news about the Colby Agency and more, check out my Web site, www.DebraWebb.com.

Enjoy!

Debra Webb

AUTHOR NOTE

Victoria Colby-Camp has stood alone at the helm of the Colby Agency for more than two decades. She survived the abduction of her son, her only child, and the brutal murder of her husband. Despite the pain and the numerous efforts of her enemies, she held her ground and remained steadfast. After years of loneliness, she fell in love with the one man who knew her better than she knew herself—Lucas Camp. She survived the return of her son. Opened her heart to the savage man he had become and helped him heal.

After twenty long years of not knowing if her son was dead or alive, her family was whole again. A grandchild brought new joy and gave Victoria hope for the kind of happiness she had not dared to dream of in the past. Yet, a woman whose agency has helped hundreds locate loved ones, find resolution to their dilemmas and obtain happiness makes more than a few enemies along the way—as her beloved first husband did in his life and as her only son has done in his. Just last year a threat to Victoria's granddaughter shook her to the core.

In true Victoria fashion, she and her venerable staff at the Colby Agency stamped out the evil that threatened. Victoria will never allow evil to triumph as long as she is breathing.

But how much longer will she continue breathing? The Colby Agency is under siege...turn the page and begin the first of six Harlequin Intrigue books that will reveal the fight for survival.

CAST OF CHARACTERS

Slade Convoy—As a Colby Agency investigator, Slade is on the side of what is just and right. He is the first investigator to be thrust into new territory that will ultimately have him breaking the law.

Mia Dawson—As former DA Gordon's personal assistant she knows too much. She had hoped to amass enough evidence to bring him down…but he may be on to her.

Former District Attorney Timothy Gordon—He's retired. He isn't about to pay for the past…but the past has other plans.

Victoria Colby-Camp—The head of the Colby Agency. When the agency is overtaken, she must do all within her power to protect her staff.

Ian Michaels—One of Victoria's seconds-in-command. As one of only two staff members not taken captive, he must do whatever necessary to keep all those inside—including his own wife—safe.

Jim Colby—Victoria's son. The next twenty-four hours prove an emotional turning point for him.

Lucas Camp—Victoria's husband. He must help find a way to rescue his wife and her staff.

Nicole Reed-Michaels—She works with Victoria to help keep the rest of the hostages calm and cooperative.

The man in charge—His identity is unknown but his ruthless tactics keep all involved on the edge of their seats.

The shackled man—His identity is unknown as well. But somehow there is a plan for him. Victoria and Nicole are certain this plan involves his death.

Chapter One

Colby Agency, Chicago
Monday, January 20, 7:45 a.m.

"Victoria."

Victoria Colby-Camp looked up from the Monday-morning briefing agenda she had prepared and smiled for the investigator waiting in her open door. "Good morning, Nicole. Did you have a nice weekend?"

Nicole Reed-Michaels moved across the office and settled into a chair in front of Victoria's desk. "I did, indeed." Nicole's lips slid into a pleasant upward tilt. "Ian and I discussed the possibility of a vacation this year." Her gaze searched Victoria's. "One that doesn't include the children."

"Ah," Victoria said, understanding now, "a second honeymoon." Ian and Nicole had been married for nine years. Two children, both school age, and their work had been the couple's focus for nearly a decade. It was past time the two took some alone time for themselves. Victoria was more than a little pleased to learn this news. "No one deserves it more." She didn't have to say that she knew this from experience. Victoria had long denied her own needs for her work and her family. "That's excellent news. Do you have a particular destination or time frame in mind?"

Nicole relaxed fully into her chair. Before coming to work at the Colby Agency she had served with the Federal Bureau of Investigation. No one should be fooled by her silky blond hair or that tall, runway physique. Nicole Reed-Michaels was not only extremely intelligent, but she was also an expert marksman and she knew how to take down an assailant with her bare hands. She was one of the agency's very best investigators. Not to mention she was married to Ian Michaels, Victoria's longtime second-in-command.

Another of those warm smiles appeared, emphasizing the tiny laugh lines that were the only indicators of age on Nicole's otherwise flawless face. "The Caribbean, I think. We're still discussing when and for how long."

"Two weeks," Victoria suggested, "at least." Before long she and Lucas would need to take a nice, indulgent vacation. They'd celebrated their sixth anniversary recently. It was time.

Last summer Victoria's son, Jim, had taken an exciting vacation to Africa with his wife, Tasha. It seemed everyone was taking vacations…except Victoria.

Yes, it was well past time.

A stifled scream echoed beyond Victoria's open door, hauling her attention there. Both she and Nicole were on their feet immediately.

"What was that?" Nicole whirled toward the sound.

Before Victoria could round her desk, Mildred burst into the office. "You've forgotten your salon appointment," she urged Victoria. "You must go *now!*" Her eyes were wide with fear.

Nicole and Victoria's gazes met briefly even as they rushed across the room.

Both knew what that seemingly silly phrase meant.

Danger had descended upon the Colby Agency. Victoria had to leave via the stairwell next to her office.

Now.

But what about Nicole? Mildred? And the others?

"Go," Nicole reaffirmed as she paused in the doorway. "I'll take care of things here."

Victoria hesitated.

"Go," Mildred repeated.

Fear expanded in Victoria's throat even as her heart threatened to rupture from her chest. She hurried through the small private lobby where Mildred greeted Victoria's appointments, opened the door to the stairwell in the narrow corridor beyond and flung herself through it.

Dear God. How could she leave everyone else behind? She should go back…assess the threat.

What was happening?

Don't think, Victoria ordered.

Go!

Her staff would need her to get through this. She couldn't help anyone with whatever situation was unfolding if she allowed herself to be overtaken. Whatever was going on…she had to escape.

Victoria hurried downward as fast as she dared. She ticked off a mental list of what she would do as soon as she was clear of the building.

Call Ian. He was off duty today. Having just completed an assignment, he had the mandatory forty-eight hours off.

Of course she would call Lucas. He had arrived home only last night from a four-day-long business trip to D.C. An hour ago she'd left him poring over the newspaper and drinking coffee. He might even be on his way here by now. He usually dropped by the agency every day that he was home.

And Jim. Dear God, she had to call her son.

Then the police.

Victoria couldn't be sure if Mildred had had time to activate the silent alarm system that would notify the authorities.

The agency's security system was state-of-the-art. As was the entire building's for that matter. Why hadn't the security guards alerted her to the threat? Both men had been at their posts in the lobby when she arrived half an hour ago.

"Good morning, ma'am."

Victoria drew up short as she reached the landing on the second floor. Only one more floor to go…but she wouldn't make it.

Dread congealed in her stomach.

The man dressed in black, including a ski-type mask to keep his face hidden, held a weapon aimed directly at her chest.

"We should return to your office, Mrs. Colby-Camp," he said quite cordially. "I'd hate for you to miss the opening act of the show."

Fury whipped through Victoria, taming her fear and stiffening her spine. "What the hell do you want?"

"Let's not get ahead of ourselves now." He gestured with the weapon for her to get moving. "Back up the stairs, ma'am."

Determination instantly replaced the dread, fueling the fury building inside her. "Not until you tell me what you want and who you are."

The evil bastard had the gall to laugh. "You've been in this business a long time, Victoria. I'm certain you've been faced with all kinds of situations and all sorts of people." Those vile lips split into a grin. "I'll bet that on occasion you've even run in to someone you really wish you hadn't messed with…." His gaze bored into hers, relaying just how little he cared whether she lived or died. "Well, that someone is me."

Chapter Two

7:57 a.m.

He was going to be late this morning.

Slade Convoy didn't actually have to be at work today, but the excitement of closing another case had to be shared. And no one understood that better than his colleagues at the Colby Agency.

His last case had been a tough one. A missing child and dysfunctional parents. The agency had been contacted by the child's paternal grandparents. Seven days missing, the child was presumed by many to be dead. Slade himself had had his doubts about finding her alive.

A triumphant smile slid across his lips. But he'd found her, very much alive. Right where her bipolar mother had hidden her.

The child was back with her father under the supervision of loving grandparents. All was right in their world once more.

The story had to be shared. He had to bask in the glory of victory with the folks who had become his family. The only family he'd ever had, really.

Slade shook off the ugly thoughts and focused on maneuvering the Magnificent Mile. As a kid he'd never imagined that one day he would work in the area. He'd considered himself lucky to have a decent meal before bedtime each night.

Life was good…now.

He appreciated every single moment.

His cell vibrated as he slowed for a traffic signal. He tucked his fingers into his pocket and fished out the phone.

He glanced at the screen and immediately recognized Ian Michaels's number. Ian was his boss. One of them anyway. Ian and Simon Ruhl were at the top of the Colby Agency food chain. Victoria ran the show, but never without the input of those two.

Slade slid the phone open. "What's up?" Strange, Slade thought, that Ian would call at this hour. Ian had bragged that today he intended to do something special with his kids.

"We have a situation."

Ian Michaels wasn't one to mince words and his tone was always calm and reserved. The man never lost his cool. Never raised his voice. And never, ever backed down or sugarcoated anything. He was about as soft as an eight-pound sledgehammer. But Slade could tell from Ian's tone something was wrong.

Slade shifted his foot to the accelerator

as the light changed to green. Whatever the situation, it was bad. Very bad.

"A situation?" Slade returned.

"Meet me at Maggie's across the street from the agency. I'll be waiting on the second floor."

"I'm close. Be there in a sec," Slade assured him. The connection ended so he slid the phone closed and tucked it back into the pocket of his jeans as he scouted for a parking slot on a side street. Maggie's Coffee House had once been a ritzy restaurant that had slowly shifted focus over the years to become a street-level café. The second floor of the artsy coffeehouse that had once been a private dining room was now used mainly for storage.

Why the hell would Ian be waiting there?

After parking his four-wheel-drive truck, Slade double-timed it up the sidewalk toward the front entrance of

Maggie's. He hesitated when he saw a familiar face heading in the same direction from the street.

"Lucas?"

Lucas Camp stopped, one hand on the door leading into Maggie's. "Convoy," the older man acknowledged, obviously not surprised.

This was getting more bizarre by the moment. Lucas was Victoria's husband, but he wasn't on the staff of the Colby Agency. Slade hustled over to the door. "What's going on?"

Lucas shook his head. "I don't know the details yet. Ian asked that I meet him here ASAP." A glimpse of worry flashed in the man's eyes before he moved forward, leading the way through the door. At the hostess's questioning look, Lucas gestured toward the stairs beyond the serving counter. She nodded as if she understood exactly what was going on.

Slade sure as hell wished he knew what was going on as he climbed the stairs behind Lucas. Well into his sixties, Lucas was damned fit, but he'd lost a leg in a long-ago war and the prosthesis he wore slowed him down a bit. But Lucas Camp didn't need any sympathy from Slade or anyone else. The man could be lethal when the need arose. He'd worked numerous deep-cover operations with the CIA for years. Even since retiring he still returned to D.C. monthly to advise the agency on the best way to conduct upcoming operations.

On the second floor, the big single room was cluttered with boxes of paper goods. Across the room near the windows overlooking the Mag Mile, Ian Michaels waited. He turned to face the new arrivals and there was no mistaking the grim expression he wore.

Whatever was going down, it was bad.

"What's going on, Ian?" Lucas demanded as he and Slade weaved their way through the stacks of boxes.

"Jim is on his way," Ian advised, avoiding a direct answer to the question.

Slade stared at the building across the street as he neared Ian's position. His gaze zeroed in on the windows of the floor where the Colby Agency suite of offices should have been buzzing with activity. It was Monday morning after all. From the outside the situation appeared to be like any other snowy January day. No smoke billowing, no shattered glass, no official emergency vehicles in the vicinity of the building. What could be wrong?

"That's good," Lucas said in response to Ian's statement regarding Jim, "but that doesn't answer my question."

Ian shifted his attention to the windows of the Colby Agency offices Slade still surveyed. "At seven forty-five this morning, a group of armed men dressed as SWAT agents laid siege to the agency and everyone inside."

"That's…crazy…." A chill penetrated deep into Slade's bones. Mondays were early days. The weekly briefing. Not only was Victoria—Lucas's wife and the head of the agency—in there, but so was every single member of the staff except for Slade and Ian…including Ian's wife, Nicole.

"How many men?" Lucas asked the question before Slade could gather his wits and utter the same.

With an uncharacteristic shake of his head, Ian turned once more to face them. "I don't know for certain. Nicole managed to get a call through to my cell but she was cut off before…" He swallowed with difficulty. "Before she could fully assess the situation. She mentioned five, then seven. But there could be more."

The same terror humming beneath

Ian's tone had claimed the usually un-readable expression on Lucas's face. "Was Nicole aware of any injuries?"

"She didn't get a chance to relay anything more."

"The security guards on duty have most likely been neutralized," Slade suggested, now visually measuring the front entrance. He hoped no one had been killed but there was always that possibility. Anyone else from the businesses housed on the other floors who might have opted to go into work early that morning had likely been taken prisoner or were dead. "We should call LSS and have them issue a warning to stay clear of the building."

LSS, Lockdown Security Systems, were the folks in charge of the building's physical security.

"That was going to be my next—"

"That was the first call I received this morning," Ian said, cutting off Lucas.

"LSS called to inform me that the building was in lockdown mode due to a gas leak and no one was to enter until the all clear was given. Before I could question the directive or pass along that the agency already had people inside, Nicole's call came in."

Lucas surveyed the building in question once more. "I don't see any official vehicles. No city maintenance crews."

"I assume the so-called leak was a ploy to enact lockdown. I've had no further word from LSS so I have to assume someone is running interference there."

Ian was right. Whoever had set this game in motion had done their homework. "Have you called the Chicago P.D.?" Slade asked. Since there were no cruisers in the vicinity he imagined the answer was no, but Ian could certainly have informed one of the agency's many contacts within Chicago P.D. to come in dark. The real SWAT folks could be on standby out of sight.

"That's not a move I want to make until I fully comprehend the terms of this situation."

Understandable. Until the terms were known, their hands were tied to a great degree.

"What's happening, Lucas?"

All three turned as Jim Colby crossed the room. The man hadn't made a sound on the stairs. Slade never ceased to be impressed by Victoria's son. He'd been trained as a mercenary as a boy. Could kill a man in mere seconds with nothing but his bare hands. As tall and muscled as he was, he could still move as stealthily as any predator of the jungle.

Lucas quickly explained what little Ian knew at this point. The fury that started to throb in Jim's temples warned that he would not stand by and wait for terms. Slade wanted to act as well. But, as Ian had shown already, this was the time for patience and levelheadedness. Jim Colby possessed neither.

"I'll assemble my team," Jim announced. "We'll move in within the hour."

Jim ran a private investigations shop. But his staff worked around the law more often than not. They called themselves the Equalizers. In sharp contrast, the Colby Agency maintained a stellar reputation, going to great lengths to cooperate fully with law enforcement. Victoria and Jim didn't see eye to eye on the way business was to be conducted.

"No."

The single syllable echoed in the silence that followed. Only two men on this planet had the guts to stare Victoria's son in the eye and tell him no: Lucas Camp and the one who'd just said the word—Ian Michaels. This was about to get hairy.

"If we're not going in," Jim growled, his gaze narrowing with the rage climbing inside him, "then what are you suggesting we do?"

"We do nothing," Ian said flatly, "until we know what the terms of this takeover are. Any step we take might be the wrong one. We wait for the man in charge to make his demands."

Jim walked two steps away, his hands planted on his hips, apparently to regain some measure of control. Or maybe to mentally pull together an entrance strategy.

Lucas took a breath. "Jim," he said as calmly and quietly as could be expected under the circumstances, "Ian has a valid point. We have to think tactically here. Allowing an emotional reaction could cause more harm than good."

Jim glared at his stepfather, then at Ian. "Reacting is not my specialty. This calls for action. *Now.*" He said the last with a pointed stare at Ian. "Waiting will only allow the intruders to gain a stronger foothold."

Ian's grim expression remained in place as he held the other man's lethal glare. "I am Victoria's second-in-command. I am and will continue to be in charge. We will proceed with caution."

Jim reclaimed the steps he'd taken, putting him toe-to-toe with Ian. "Victoria is my mother. We'll do things my way. No negotiations."

Slade shared a look with Lucas. The circumstances were sensitive to say the least. Both men were strong-willed and each had a legitimate point. But, as a staff member of the Colby Agency, Slade's alliance had to be with Ian. Jim was operating solely on emotion. Bad business at a moment like this.

Lucas stepped between the two men, forcing both to take a much-needed step back. "Everyone in this room has a vested interest in how this turns out." He glanced at Jim, then at Ian. "We will all remain calm and we will lay out a proper strategy. There will be no going in blind or taking unnecessary risks before we have a single detail to go on."

Slade relaxed marginally. If anyone could control this out-of-control moment, Lucas could.

The chirp of a cell phone shattered the tense silence.

Ian reached into the pocket of his suit jacket and pulled out his cell. "Michaels."

A muscle throbbed in Jim's hard-set jaw. Lucas stared hopefully at Ian. Slade waited, also hoping that this would be some kind of news. A first move.

Time was slipping by. Every second that lapsed could be one that may have been pivotal to saving one or more lives. The lives of people Slade knew and cared for deeply. Whatever happened, in all probability the Colby Agency would never be the same.

"Yes," Ian said, "I understand." He drew the phone from his ear and touched the screen. "As requested, you are on speakerphone."

Adrenaline moved through Slade's veins.

"Fourteen staff members as well as Victoria Colby-Camp are now my hostages," the male voice announced. "All communications inside the building, including the Internet, cell phones and landlines, have been disabled. The building is stalled in lockdown mode and under my control. No one gets in or out. If anyone tries, the hostages will die. If the authorities, local or federal, are contacted, the hostages will die."

No one made a sound or even breathed. The distant hum of conversation and coffee mugs sliding across tables and counters from below were the only sounds.

"Are you prepared to issue your demands for the release of the hostages?" Ian inquired with amazing calm and self-assurance.

Jim looked away, the fury now visibly pulsing across his brow.

"There are only two."

Only two. *Great,* Slade mused.

All four men waited for the harsh nightmare to become a stone-cold reality.

"Former District Attorney Timothy Gordon will be brought, by whatever means necessary, to the front entrance of the building. This demand is nonnegotiable."

Now Slade got the picture. This wasn't about the Colby Agency at all. It was about one of Chicago's most prestigious political figures.

"Is it your intent to exchange the

hostages for Gordon?" Ian asked, his tone still incredibly calm.

"I have two demands, Mr. Michaels," the man said, his voice equally calm and absolutely firm. "When you have met this first demand, we will discuss the status of the hostages as well as the next step."

"This is Lucas Camp," the oldest of those gathered in the storeroom asserted. "Before we go any further, we will need proof of life. And a detailed listing of the physical condition of all hostages."

The caller made a sound, not really a laugh but something on that order. "We have three injuries, none life-threatening. But, Mr. Camp, if you're asking about the condition of your wife, she is indeed among the injured."

Jim swore loudly. Ian and Lucas shot him a glare. Slade moved to Jim's side, placed a hand on his arm and urged him with his eyes to stay calm. The slightest wrong move or comment could set off a chain reaction no one wanted.

"Under the circumstances," Ian offered, "we must demand that you release the injured hostages before we proceed with negotiations."

The sound that echoed in the air was an outright laugh this time. "Mr. Michaels, this is a one-way negotiation. You will bring Gordon to the front entrance. As I've already explained, we will discuss the release of the hostages at that point and not a moment sooner."

"You," Jim warned, stepping forward, "have made a grave mistake. Release the hostages now and we'll forget this ever happened. Refuse and you have my word that your life will never again be your own."

"You have sixty seconds to agree to this demand."

Shock throbbed in the silence that followed.

"If you do not agree to this demand in the next fifty-five seconds," the voice demanded when no one responded, "one of the hostages will die."

"This is—" Ian began.

"Fifty seconds," the man on the phone interrupted. "Another hostage will die with each minute that passes after that."

More of that choking silence.

"Forty seconds, gentlemen. Perhaps I'll start with one of the females." There was a muffled sound followed by the caller shouting to one of his cohorts, "Bring me the deaf woman. I doubt anyone will really miss her."

Slade held his breath. Dear God…

"We will do everything in our power," Ian said, shattering the tension, "to meet your demand."

"Not good enough, Michaels," the voice warned. "Thirty seconds."

"How long do we have to bring Gordon to you?" Jim roared.

Ian looked from Lucas to Jim as if he wanted to argue, but fear for his wife as well as the others kept him from voicing his concerns.

"Twenty-three hours and nineteen minutes. You will deliver D.A. Gordon to the front entrance of the building by seven forty-five tomorrow morning or everyone dies. And I do mean everyone."

"He'll be there," Jim announced. "You have my word."

"Remember, gentlemen," the voice cautioned, "any contact with the authorities, any attempts to gain entrance to the building, and everyone dies."

"You have my word," Jim repeated without reservation. "Gordon will be there on time as requested. We will cooperate fully with all your terms."

"Excellent. I'm always relieved when no one has to die. But," the man added, his voice pulsating with pure evil, "I will without remorse execute one hostage after the other until they're all dead if the need arises. My men will disappear as quickly and untraceably as they appeared. Just like smoke. Do we understand each other?"

"Perfectly," Jim stated.

The connection was severed. Ian immediately started entering numbers on the keypad of his cell. Jim stopped him. "What're you doing?"

"Determining if I can track the call back to a traceable number."

Jim snatched the cell out of his hand. Fury glistened in Ian's eyes.

"We will contact no one," Jim told him in no uncertain terms. "We will deliver Gordon just as he requested."

Again Lucas intervened. "Convoy will get to work on rounding up Gordon," he suggested. "Ian and I will attempt to get to the bottom of who's behind this takeover."

"And my people," Jim said, "will determine if there is a way inside without detection."

Three, then five seconds of traumatic silence elapsed.

"Agreed," Ian said, capitulating.

"Agreed," Lucas chimed in.

All three looked to Slade. He held up his hands. "I'm ready to do whatever needs to be done."

"Good." Jim set his formidable attention on Slade. "Find Gordon. Bring him in."

Not exactly the easiest job he'd ever been assigned. "What if he doesn't want to cooperate?" Slade felt the question was a legitimate one.

"Do whatever is necessary," Jim told him. "Just get him here."

Slade hesitated to see if Ian would object. When he didn't, Slade shrugged. "No problem."

Chapter Three

Inside the Colby Agency, 8:50 a.m.

Victoria tightened her lips against the moan that welled in her throat. Her head throbbed and nausea roiled in her stomach.

She couldn't show the first sign of weakness. The others were depending upon her.

All fourteen of her staff members had been shoved into the conference room. Two others were injured as well. Thankfully none appeared to be life-threatening.

"Victoria."

She drew in a deep breath and forced a calm into her voice that she by no means felt. "I'm all right," she assured Nicole. "We're all going to be all right. I'm certain Ian, Lucas and Jim are doing all within their power to regain control of the situation."

Merri Walters most likely had a mild concussion, at the very least a contusion. Victoria ached for the woman. Unable to hear the approach of the bastards who had taken control of the Colby Agency, Merri hadn't reacted rapidly enough. She'd gotten a brutal whack to the back of the head for the delay. But she was coherent and, mercifully, showed no outward signs of serious trouble.

Fury vibrated through Victoria. Whatever these animals wanted, they would be sorry they had chosen the Colby Agency as their target.

She would see to that. *Somehow.*

Nicole glanced at Merri and the others

huddled around her. "She seems okay." Her attention shifted to the newest investigator on the Colby staff, Kendra Todd. The swelling and bruises on her face reminded all the others that back talk would not be permitted. "But I'll need to keep an eye on Kendra. She isn't accustomed to being pushed around."

Several of the men, Ted Tallant and Trinity Barrett in particular, had their share of swelling, bruises and scrapes for having attempted to fight off the attack while the rest, Victoria included, ran for exits.

Their captors had been prepared for just such a diversion. Both fire exits had been covered and the elevators had been locked down.

"You monitor Kendra and help Simon with the others," Victoria agreed. "I'm going to see if I can learn the shackled prisoner's identity." He was the one unknown variable in this equation.

Nicole's gaze followed Victoria's to the man on the other side of the room. He'd been dragged into the conference room and shackled to a chair as far away from Victoria's staff as possible within the confines of the same four walls. A cloth sack covered his face and head, and his plain gray sweatshirt and worn jeans gave no indication of who he was or where he'd come from. The generic sneakers he wore had seen far better days. There was nothing about his appearance or his bearing that gave the slightest impression of who he was. He hadn't attempted to speak or escape, which could mean he was either gagged or drugged. Not that escape was an option considering the way his ankles and wrists were bound together and his waist was manacled to the chair. His head drooped forward as if he were in fact unconscious.

"His guard doesn't look too friendly," Nicole commented under her breath.

That much was true. The guard wore black like all the others, including the concealing ski mask. The weapon in his hand indicated he didn't trust anyone enough to holster it. Though all visible beyond the mask were his dark eyes, that glimpse into his psyche warned that he wasn't taking any chances or any grief.

"The least I can do is try," Victoria insisted as she struggled from her position on the floor to her feet. Her head swam. She braced against the wall to steady herself. She'd made the mistake of struggling with the two men who had escorted her to this room. Being made an example of wasn't a surprise—she'd expected as much. Her attackers had wanted to ensure all present realized that Victoria was no longer in control. Several of her staff members had gotten roughed up when they'd attempted to come to her aid. All the more reason she had to tread carefully. Her staff would be taking their cues from her.

Their safety depended a great deal on her every action.

Even as the thought echoed in her brain, she slowly crossed the room toward the shackled man and his personal guard. She'd already spotted the tracks of dried blood down the front of his sweatshirt. He no doubt needed medical attention the same as she did and many of her staff members.

"Back on the floor," the man with the gun ordered. He shifted the business end of his weapon in her direction to reinforce his order.

Victoria halted. "He's bleeding." She gestured to the mysterious prisoner. "I just want to check to see that he's not seriously injured. He may need medical attention."

The guard scoffed. "He'll be dead soon enough. Any injuries he sustained are inconsequential."

Victoria refused to flinch. "Surely you don't mean to deprive us of proper care for our injuries, and some water." She indicated the door on the other side of the room. "There's bottled water and coffee in the lounge across the hall. And first-aid supplies." If someone made a run for it, it couldn't be her. She would not leave a single member of her staff behind. Perhaps Nicole would be allowed to go across the hall. She could attempt an escape if the opportunity presented itself.

This very minute Lucas, Ian and Jim would be planning how to resolve this takeover. These bastards had no idea how lucky they would be to survive the coming battle.

"Sit down," the guard ordered. "Or—" he shifted his aim toward the others huddled around Merri "—one of them dies."

Victoria backed up a step. "Fine. I'll sit." She couldn't take the risk that he might not be bluffing. "But you, sir, should think about how to keep your hostages from further harm. We're no good to you unless we're alive."

His glare was his only response.

The unidentified prisoner was apparently unconscious. She hadn't heard a moan or any other sort of sound from him. If he'd been awake and aware of himself, he would surely have tried to communicate as Victoria had questioned the guard about him.

As she settled on the floor near the members of her staff, she and Nicole exchanged a look of defeat.

No. Victoria refused to be defeated. Not by these men. Not by anyone. True, she had lost that battle, but she wasn't through by a long shot.

Simon Ruhl, one of her most trusted investigators and one of her seconds-in-command, kept one arm around Merri as she leaned against his shoulder. He flashed a ghost of a smile at Victoria. She understood what the gesture meant. They would be okay. Lucas, Ian and Jim would not fail. They would find a way to neutralize the hostiles. Simon's confidence affirmed her own.

All Victoria and her people had to do was remain patient and cooperate with these infiltrators. This day, this nightmare, would soon be reversed. The most brilliant minds on the planet were working together.

The conference room door abruptly flew inward. All eyes swung to the man loitering in the open doorway.

"You," the man who appeared to be in charge said to Victoria, "come with me." It was impossible to tell him apart from the others except for his voice. His accent said he wasn't an American by birth. Perhaps he was of European ancestry.

Simon and several others braced to defend Victoria, but she signaled with a small shake of her head for them to stand down.

Whatever happened to her, the most important thing was for the others to remain safe. To survive.

As Victoria dragged herself up once more and walked slowly toward the door, she tried to remember if she'd told Lucas she loved him that morning before leaving for the office. They'd shared a light kiss. That part she remembered vividly, as always.

Tears brimmed on her lashes and the ache deepened in her chest. They hadn't had nearly enough time together. She'd made him wait so very, very long.

And Jim? When they'd spoken by phone last night, had she told him how very much she loved him? Or Jamie, her sweet little granddaughter?

Victoria hoped that was the case.

She might never get the opportunity again.

Chapter Four

Treamont condo complex, 9:20 a.m.

Mia Dawson checked her reflection in the mirror once more. She could do this. No matter that he was most likely on to her.

She could do it.

No one else had the level of access she did. If she failed to get this done…then he would just get away with his crimes.

It was her duty as a citizen of Chicago—as a human being—to see that he was stopped. And she owed it to her cousin to ensure justice prevailed.

Mia took a deep breath, moistened her lips and strengthened her determination.

There was no one else. It had to be her.

Grabbing her purse and keys on the way to the front door, she pushed aside the fear and reached for the door. She could do this.

A fist pounding on the slab of wood shook the doorknob in her hand.

She blinked, resisted the impulse to draw back a step. It wouldn't be him or one of his men. She was on her way to his home now. He would much rather carry out any confrontation on his own turf.

Just check the security peephole and see who it is.

Mia leaned forward and took a look. A tall man with blond hair stood on the other side of her door. A frown furrowed her brow. She'd never seen this man before. She squinted, looked again. No, he was a stranger. Knowing her boss, he could have hired someone new just for this job.

Taking care of the enemy.

She swallowed back the uncertainty,

deliberately slowed her breathing. "Who is it?" No point in pretending she wasn't home. If he'd been sent to take care of her, he would know she wasn't at work and that her car remained in the underground parking garage.

"I'm Investigator Slade Convoy. I have a few questions for you related to your work with former district attorney Timothy Gordon."

Holy hell. She searched her brain, tried to reason what his statement meant. Seemed damned coincidental that an investigator would show up at her door at precisely this moment.

"Do you have some ID?" IDs could be faked, but asking felt like the right thing to do. He would surely expect her to ask.

The man shoved a credentials case close to the peephole. The case was open so that the identification card was displayed.

The Colby Agency. Private Investigator Slade Convoy.

The Colby Agency. The name rang a bell. She'd heard it at some point. Maybe on a case her boss had prosecuted. Maybe from a defendant. She stiffened her posture and demanded, "Why would you want to talk to me? Who sent you?" The latter was the far better question. *If* he told the truth.

"Ma'am, I really don't want to do this in the hallway. The subject matter is sensitive."

Ah, he avoided the important question altogether. Getting inside was his objective. "Who did you say sent you?" she repeated, though he hadn't said at all.

"Victoria Colby-Camp, the head of the Colby Agency."

That name sounded familiar as well. "Is there a way I can verify that?"

Impatience etched across his face. "You can call my supervisor. His name is Ian Michaels." To her surprise, the man rattled off a number.

Mia chewed her bottom lip. What the hell? She fished her cell phone from her purse and entered the number.

After the first ring, a male voice uttered, "Michaels."

She cleared her throat. "This is Mia Dawson. There's a man at my door. His…name is Slade Convoy. He claims he represents your agency."

This made no sense! He could have given her any number. No matter what this Ian Michaels said, he could be lying as well. She wasn't thinking.

"Ms. Dawson, it would mean a great deal to the Colby Agency if you allowed Mr. Convoy to ask you a few questions. I can't divulge the nature of the situation, as you might well imagine. But your assistance is greatly needed and would be genuinely appreciated."

She had to be out of her mind to even

consider opening the door. "I'm sorry, Mr. Michaels, but you and Mr. Convoy are asking me to open my door to a complete stranger. I'm certain you can understand how unwise such a move would be."

"I do understand, Ms. Dawson." He paused. "I don't want to frighten you, but this is a matter of life and death. Without your help, fifteen people stand to lose their lives."

Good Lord. How did she say no to that? Would anyone go that far to gain access to her when all he had to do was wait for her in the basement near or inside her vehicle? "All right. I'll…talk to him." Michaels thanked her before she disconnected. She had to admit that he sounded genuinely sincere.

Mia peered out the security hole once more. "Mr. Convoy, remove your jacket, please, so that I can see whether or not you're armed."

The man rolled his eyes but acquiesced to her demand. He removed the lined leather coat he wore and dropped it to the floor. Then he held up both hands, surrender style, and turned all the way around so that she could ensure there was no weapon tucked into his waistband.

When he faced the door again, he dropped his arms to his sides. "Satisfied?"

Another moment of hesitation lapsed before she relented and opened the door. He stood before her, taller than he'd looked through the tiny hole. One more deep breath. "How can I help you?"

He gestured to the room behind her. "Surely you can understand how I wouldn't want to have this discussion in a public corridor like this."

No way was this man getting her alone inside her condo. "Since I don't know the nature of your business, I'll have to disagree. What can I do for you, sir?" She'd made all the compromises so far—time for him to make one.

Tension started to throb in his square jaw. If he was one of her boss's thugs, he was damned good-looking. She gave herself a mental shake. What the hell was wrong with her?

"Fine." The tightening of his lips warned that he wasn't happy. "The Colby Agency is investigating Mr. Gordon. I'm hoping you can clear up a couple of things for us before we make a wrong step. Whatever you tell me will be completely off the record. No one will connect any of it back to you."

Interest stirred. Gordon was being investigated? This was the first she'd heard of that. "What sort of investigation?"

Convoy glanced around. "I'm sorry." He shook his head. "I just can't talk about this in the open like this. You're going to have to trust me."

Anticipation nudged her. This could be the break she'd been hoping for. All she had to do was take the risk. She reached into her purse and removed her pepper spray, rested her forefinger on the trigger. "Come in." Stepping back, she opened the door wider.

Convoy picked up his coat and crossed her threshold. She hadn't noticed until then that he wore cowboy boots. Faded jeans and a striped button-up shirt. Other than the pricy jacket he didn't exactly look like any high-class investigator she'd ever met. And if she recalled correctly, the Colby Agency was no low-rent P.I. shop.

Keeping her finger ready on the trigger, Mia closed the door and turned to her visitor. "What is the nature of your investigation?"

"Our client," he began, "has requested a face-to-face with Mr. Gordon."

Mia shrugged. "Gordon has a secretary. I'm certain a simple phone call is all you'd need to set up an appointment for your client." Mia wasn't the man's secretary. She'd been his personal assistant for two years, had the rest of this month to go and then they were done. A tingle of fear shimmered through her. Less than one month to go to get what she needed. She was so close, but close wouldn't cut it. The evidence had to be in her possession before she made her next move.

And that all depended upon whether or not he was on to her extracurricular activities.

Convoy glanced around the room. "I'm afraid the usual route for this sort of thing won't work. Our client wants this meeting off the record as well."

A new kind of fear reared its ugly head. "What does that mean?" Good grief, she'd been so fired up to get the goods on Gordon, she very well may have walked into a trap. But what kind of trap? What was the Colby Agency after? Who was this client he kept referring to?

His gaze, the shade so intensely green that it made her quiver, zeroed in on hers. "I'm going to cut right to the chase, Ms. Dawson."

"That would be nice." She braced, mentally and physically.

"We have a hostage situation at the Colby Agency. Contacting the authorities is out of the question. If I don't bring Gordon in for this little tête-à-tête, then folks are going to die. I have only a few hours to accomplish that task."

Mia hadn't seen anyone else in the corridor outside her door. This man was alone. No cameras. No audio recorders visible. He was unarmed, for heaven's sake. Yet, this had to be some kind of scam or setup. It was too bizarre to be real. Mia Dawson had never believed in coincidences.

Not to mention what he was talking about was kidnapping. A felony.

"O-kay." She felt her gaze narrow. "What's going on here? I don't know what you're up to, but you can tell me the truth now or I'm calling the police." Her free hand went instinctively to her cell phone while her forefinger settled more fully on the pepper spray trigger. This game was over.

"Wait." He held up both hands as she produced her cell. "I'm telling the truth," he urged. "I don't know what else to say to convince you, but this is not a scam or a joke. It's real and people are going to die."

Maybe if he hadn't looked dead serious—or if she didn't want to get her boss so badly—she wouldn't have hesitated.

Could she really have gotten so lucky

that an avenue to execute her plans had fallen right into her lap?

"You want me to believe you?" She hiked up her chin in defiance of the skepticism simmering beneath the hope. "Take me to the Colby Agency and let me hear this from someone besides a voice on the telephone."

His hands dropped impotently to his sides once more. "That's the one thing I can't do." That unsettling gaze pierced hers once more. "The truth is, ma'am, I could have waited for you in your little hybrid in the garage. I could have taken you by force. But I'm giving you the opportunity to do the right thing on your own."

Her head was moving from side to side in protest before he completed the discourse on how this was the best for her. "If you need my help to do something that's clearly illegal, then you're going to have to show me that the stakes are as you say." She wasn't stupid. This guy had to be out of his mind if he thought she was going to go along with this crazy plan without some sort of tangible proof.

He thought about her demand for a moment, that tension still keeping a furious rhythm in his jaw. "Going to the agency is impossible. That's where the hostages are being held. But I can take you to the temporary command center we've set up."

"Who's holding the hostages? If someone wants a face-to-face with Gordon, it must be an old enemy of his." That was the only plausible explanation. As much as she wanted to see the scumbag go down, she would not be responsible for turning him over to some recently released criminal he'd once prosecuted. She was already only weeks from being without a job, she wasn't going to make tracks to prison as well.

The unemployment line was unpalatable enough.

Slade Convoy was the one shaking his head now. "We don't know the answer to that question just yet. Our people, what's left of them, are attempting to determine the source of the threat. Right now we have no choice but to accede to the demand given. Time is not on our side."

This was one of those moments... when a woman had to decide if she was going to take an obvious leap of faith for what she believed in or just allow an opportunity to pass right on by.

This man...Slade Convoy...and the agency he represented didn't have to know about her own agenda. This could actually work to her benefit. "I suppose that's reasonable." She had to be a lot desperate or a little crazy to go along with this. But she knew Gordon better than anyone else. She might even be able to help with determining who was behind this takeover. "I can also give you a list of the cases he has prosecuted the past couple of years. Your threat may be coming from one of those."

The relief that flashed in the investigator's eyes was palpable. "I'll inform my superior that we're on our way."

If Gordon was on to what she was up to, she was likely on more than one hit list already. Why not take a risk? One that might ensure she survived?

Not daring to return the canister of pepper spray to her purse, she held on to it with her left hand while she adjusted the shoulder strap of her purse with her right. "Fine. But keep in mind that I'm going to be late for work as it is. With Gordon," she added sharply.

"In that case," Convoy said, gesturing to the door, "what're we waiting for?"

Mia bit her lips together. For a way out of this, she didn't say.

For someone to save her…from herself.

Chapter Five

Maggie's Coffee House, 10:40 a.m.

Slade nodded to one of the waitresses as he weaved his way between customers and behind the counter. The stairs to the second floor were behind a door marked Employees Only. He held it open for Mia, and she hesitated long enough to meet his eyes.

She still wasn't sure about this. The fact of the matter was he'd expected to have to bring her here by force. He should be thankful he hadn't been obliged to take extreme measures. This whole situation was way out of control and rushing well beyond previously re-spected legal boundaries.

As she ascended the narrow stairs, he considered that besides a great-looking backside, the woman had the bluest eyes he'd ever seen. Like the darkest depths of the ocean. She looked younger than he'd expected. Rather than the twenty-nine her dossier revealed, she looked more like twenty-one. But that couldn't be right. She'd graduated at the top of her class at Northwestern and had worked five years in the Cook County District Attorney's office, two for Gordon himself. Slade wondered why she'd never opted to go to law school. From what he'd read she was damned good at taking care of business.

After moving only a few steps across the room, Mia stopped in her tracks.

Slade couldn't exactly blame her. Since he'd left, things had changed big-time. The boxes containing paper products had been moved to one corner. Several tables had been pushed together to make a conference center of sorts. A blueprint of the building across the street had been taped to a nearby wall. Computers hummed with the work of folks Slade didn't recognize.

Noting his frown of confusion, Ian gestured to the two guys stationed at the computers. "Jim brought a couple of his team members to support our efforts."

Jim Colby, Victoria's son, stared out the windows as if by sheer force of will he could free his mother from the siege that had descended upon the Colby Agency only three hours ago.

"This is Mia Dawson." Slade indicated the woman at his side, then his superior. "Ian Michaels, the Colby Agency's second-in-command."

"Ms. Dawson." Ian approached and extended his hand. "We sincerely appreciate your cooperation under the circumstances."

"Is that because what you're doing is against a number of laws?" Mia demanded, obviously deciding to cut to the chase.

Both Jim and Lucas, Victoria's husband, turned from their station at the window to assess the woman who'd issued such a vehement inquiry.

Slade had a feeling Ms. Dawson had heard all she wanted to from him. Ian could take it from here. Slade had done a hell of a lot of research on the Colby Agency before accepting the position a year or so ago. The one thing that had drawn him to the offered position was the stellar reputation of Victoria Colby-Camp and her entire staff. The agency was highly respected by local law enforcement as well as those on the federal level.

The plan they had no choice but to

enact was about as far from reputable as could be gotten.

The Colby Agency stood on the verge of moving into new territory. Irreparable damage was not only possible, but it was also unavoidable.

"We have fifteen staff members, including Victoria Colby-Camp, in the building across the street." He indicated the window where Lucas and Jim still stood. "All communications have been severed. The building itself is in lockdown mode. As of this moment, we have no avenues of entrance. No negotiating chips, save one."

"Gordon," she suggested.

Ian acknowledged her suggestion with a nod. "If we contact the authorities in any capacity the hostages will die. Considering the way the infiltrators were able to shut down all communications and lock down the entire building, I'm inclined to believe their threat that they are aware of our every move."

Slade shifted his attention from Mia's full lips as she moistened them. She was nervous and rightly so. And he, apparently, hadn't taken care of his sexual urges recently. Being attracted to her at a time like this was immensely stupid.

"Which also indicates they know you've brought me into the situation," Mia added.

"No doubt."

She swore, then whipped around to glare at Slade. He blinked, trying to ignore the way her silky black hair flew around her shoulders. The woman was damned gorgeous, and equally stubborn. But neither of those traits would salvage this situation.

"This could cost me my position," she snapped.

"You're already on notice," Ian interjected. "Three or four weeks are all that remain on your contract with the D.A.'s office, correct?"

Outrage tightened her face. "That's right, but I've applied for another position with the new D.A. This kind of move could jeopardize my chances of a new contract."

Ian nodded once more. "Not helping us could cost the lives of fifteen people."

"Including his wife," Slade said quietly. "The mother of his children."

Ian stabbed him with a deadly glare.

"My God," Mia mumbled.

Lucas Camp ambled across the room. "Ms. Dawson, I'm Lucas Camp." He shook the hand she offered, however limply. "Victoria is my wife," he confessed, "but this isn't about that. All fifteen of the Colby employees inside that building are someone's wife or husband, son or daughter. Most are mothers or fathers. Above all else, they're innocent victims of the madman behind this. The only connection, the one avenue for helping them, is Mr. Gordon."

Mia's chest rose and fell with a big breath. Slade gave himself a mental kick for observing that move far too closely. Maybe he needed another day of R & R to clear his head.

"What is it you want me to do?" Mia's compassion overwhelmed the anger and mistrust.

"I'm sure Gordon won't come here willingly," Ian explained. "Certainly he wouldn't threaten his own safety without involving the authorities."

A laugh burst from Mia's lips. Every gaze in the room landed on her. "Are you kidding? He wouldn't threaten his safety for his own mother, much less anyone else's."

Ian and Lucas exchanged a look.

"That's why we need you," Slade ventured. "My job is to make my way into his estate and bring him here... whether he wants to come or not."

Big blue eyes widened. "Are you serious? You want to kidnap him?"

"That's one way to put it," Slade acknowledged.

Jim's foreboding presence abruptly muscled between the men gathered around Mia. "We're not asking your permission here, Ms. Dawson. We're going to do this with or without your agreement."

Slade's attention shot to Ian. Jim's heavy-handedness was a major hot button with Ian.

Purse still hanging from her shoulders, Mia planted her hands on her hips. "You're saying I don't have a choice?" she demanded, staring at Jim Colby. "That I either help you or what? You'll kill me or something?"

"No, Ms. Dawson, certainly not," Ian said quickly. "We feel certain that under the circumstances you'll want to cooperate with our efforts. We will ensure that

Mr. Gordon's safety is protected at all times. We won't send him in, under any circumstances, unless we have backup in place."

"How the hell can you promise that?" Jim demanded. His hands hung at his sides and were clenched in fury. "We'll do whatever we have to."

"I'll take Ms. Dawson downstairs for coffee," Slade suggested. He was relatively certain Ian did not want her to witness the debate about to take place.

"No." She backed away from Slade's outstretched hand. "If you expect me to help with this, I'm going to be in on both sides of the argument."

Then she said something that shocked Slade. "Besides, what makes you think I care about Gordon's safety? The only thing I'm worried about is my future career in the D.A.'s office."

Ian's questioning gaze settled on Slade. Slade shrugged, then said to her,

"My background research didn't reveal any hostility between you and Gordon."

Mia glared at him. "You ran a background search on me? What the hell for? I don't have a criminal record and my professional record in the D.A.'s office is above reproach."

"Is there a personal relationship between you and Gordon that we're unaware of?" Ian asked with his typical frankness.

"Absolutely not," she said entirely too quickly. "I just don't care for the man, that's all. And he's history. My focus is on the future. I don't want to see anyone die for him, but I don't want to kill my career, either."

Ian was suspicious. As controlled as the man's calm facade was, Slade understood that his assessment of Mia Dawson had moved to a different level. So had Slade's, for that matter.

"Then you don't have any problem

helping Mr. Convoy obtain access to Gordon's estate?" Ian proposed.

She blinked once, twice. "If that's what you need me to do to—" she gestured vaguely to the window "—help you recover this situation."

Slade's instincts went on point. There was something more going on here. He and Ian shared another of those knowing looks.

"Let's go have that coffee now," Lucas suggested, stepping forward. "I'd like to hear more about your working relationship with Gordon."

Mia's expression gave away her uncertainty. "I'm supposed to be at his place right now. I'm helping him transfer his working note files to storage."

Lucas took her arm, wrapped it around his. "You have my word, this won't take long."

Mia didn't resist. Few people had the guts to protest anything Lucas Camp suggested. Neither his age nor his obvious limp overshadowed his ability to intimidate with a single look or word.

When the two had disappeared down the stairs, Ian turned a furious glare on Jim. "We will not send Gordon inside unless we have backup in place. I've already agreed to the *no-cops* edict. That's as far as I'm willing to cross the line on this."

"And if we can't get backup in place," Jim countered. "We're just going to sit back and let them die when the time runs out?"

The pain that flashed in Ian's eyes twisted Slade's gut into knots. "We have just over twenty hours to get someone inside," Ian summed up. "I'm certain we will be successful. Surely you don't expect Slade to drag Gordon out of his compound in broad daylight? This will need to be done after he's retired for the evening so as not to draw attention."

Ian made a valid point.

"At seven-thirty tomorrow morning," Jim said, obviously not backing off, "we will turn Gordon over, no matter our tactical situation."

"If we're waiting until later tonight," Slade asked, only just now seeing how this was going to play out for him over the next few hours, "how am I supposed to ensure Ms. Dawson doesn't have a change of heart and call the police between now and then?"

Considering he couldn't prevent her from going to work, otherwise suspicions would be roused, he couldn't be absolutely certain she wouldn't call the authorities once she was out of his line of sight.

"You'll find a way," Jim said before returning to the window.

"We're missing something," Ian said for Slade's ears only. "She's somewhat too eager. A woman who has spent the past five years working on the side of justice wouldn't suddenly be so amiable to such a plan." He glanced back at the work going on. "Watch her, Convoy. There may be an undisclosed revelation coming."

"Will do," Slade assured him.

He hustled down the stairs, visually located Lucas and Mia. He watched a moment as she sipped her coffee. Her smile was nervous but seemingly genuine.

Ian was right. She was definitely hiding something relevant to all this.

She glanced up as Slade approached. "Time to get you to work," he said, pushing aside his suspicions for the moment.

"Thank you, Mr. Camp." Mia rose from her chair. "I'll keep all you said in mind."

Slade nodded to Lucas then headed back to his truck with the single key they possessed to this incredible mess. Mia Dawson, a woman with an agenda. "What wisdom did Lucas have to offer?"

She paused at the passenger-side door of his truck. "That I had nothing to worry about. He would personally ensure the job I'd applied for was mine if I wanted it." Those long, dark lashes swept down over her eyes, quickly covering a glimpse of fear or uncertainty. "However this thing turns out."

Well, well, maybe the lady really wasn't worried about anything but her job.

The idea didn't sit comfortably in Slade's gut. Whenever a person worked so incredibly hard to ensure all were aware of his or her single goal, one thing was absolutely certain.

It wasn't the true goal at all.

Chapter Six

Gordon compound, 1:25 p.m.

Two hours had passed since Slade had watched Mia pull her small hybrid sedan through the gate of the Gordon property. Just outside of Chicago, the property reminded Slade of a compound provided for a wealthy political figure in exile. Mammoth, but closed off from the world. No amount of luxury could offset the intimidation of the twelve-foot walls and the state-of-the-art electronic security surveillance system.

Evidently the seven-figure book deal

Gordon had landed after retiring as Cook County's D.A. allowed him to step way, way up in the world.

All that money and the man couldn't escape his enemies.

Lethal enemies.

Those enemies were using the Colby Agency to lure their prey into a trap.

It was Slade's job to see that Gordon walked straight into that trap.

Five minutes more and he was scheduled to enter the compound to pick up the boxed files for transporting back to the county's file storage facility.

Ian had ensured that Slade had all he needed. A properly marked van, uniform and an authentic ID. The files would be turned over to the appropriate security guard at the facility as soon as the task was accomplished. The Colby Agency had contacts from the top on down to the lowest echelon of society, as well as professional assets. Slade never ceased to be amazed at what Ian and Simon could come up with.

Doing this right was supremely important for many reasons. One, to ensure no one died. Second, for damage control. No way was the Colby Agency coming out of this smelling like a rose.

Kidnapping was a felony.

Slade fully understood the risk he was taking.

So did Mia, it seemed.

He still didn't get the idea that she'd caved so easily to the demand.

If he were damned lucky, her cooperation was real and wouldn't come back to bite him in the backside.

So far, only a few minor laws had been broken. But the moment he drove off the compound with those files, despite the fact that he would immediately turn them over to the appropriate handler, Slade was crossing a line. The files were county property. Case files. Sensitive. Protected.

Then there was the second step in his task. Ensuring Gordon's full cooperation. Kidnapping.

Both Ian and Lucas had insisted they would take full responsibility. Jim Colby wanted to do this personally, but Lucas and Ian had convinced him that his time would be better spent focused on finding a way into the building beneath the radar of the gunmen inside.

Slade glanced at the digital clock on the dash. Time to do this. He started the engine and pulled away from the curb. Braking at the intersection, he turned right and headed for the Gordon compound.

At the gate Slade depressed the call button.

"Let's see some ID," the face and voice on the four-inch security monitor told him.

Slade tugged the clip-on badge from his shirt pocket and held it in front of the screen's built-in camera.

"When you enter the gate, drive straight back to the garage," the man, obviously a member of Gordon's private security, ordered.

"Will do." Slade clipped the badge back onto his pocket and waited for the gates to swing inward.

He rolled across the European-style pavers until he reached the garage. A long, low whistle hissed past his lips as he got a full view of the mansion Gordon called home. The building looked more like something a big-time celebrity would call home.

Slade shifted into Park and shut off the engine. "Showtime." He grabbed the jacket that matched the uniform and pulled it on as he got out. The cold January air cut through him before he could shrug the jacket into place.

The second of the three garage doors opened as he reached for the clipboard on the dash, then closed the door.

Mia stood waiting as the overhead door moved upward. "The boxes are inside." She hitched a thumb toward the massive garage behind her. "Just follow me."

Acknowledging her statement with a nod, he walked toward her. "Afternoon, ma'am."

"We…have six boxes with matching bar codes." Her voice was a little shaky, nervous. "You'll need to document that you've accepted each one."

The last thing he needed was for her to blow this. Too many lives were depending on how this went down. And this step was only phase one. "I understand, ma'am," he assured her, hoping to allay her too-evident fears.

She visually inspected him from head to toe before turning to lead the way into the house.

He surveyed the garage. Two classic luxury vehicles, each polished to a high sheen, claimed two of the parking spaces. From the yard the only means of access to the garage were the overhead doors. No walk-through door. A single paneled door, which looked to be steel, separated the garage from a mudroom and pantry-style storage area. No windows in the garage, only one in the first entry point into the home.

Slade visually assessed each room they encountered as Mia led the way to Gordon's home office beyond the kitchen and family room. They encountered none of the three security personnel she had told him would be on duty inside. Another patrolled the perimeter outside the home. At midnight, the number inside was reduced to only one. Since Slade wasn't met and patted down by security, he had to assume that Mia remained a trusted employee.

She turned back to him then, clasped her trembling hands in front of her. "Mr.

Gordon prefers that hand trucks are not used in the house, so you'll need to carry each box out to the garage."

He placed his clipboard on the first box in the stack, then lifted it into his arms. The typical boxes designed for legal-size files, each was taped securely and marked with an identifying bar code across the tape to ensure that breaking the seal would be readily visible.

Mia followed him back to the garage. Five more trips. He wondered if she planned to trace his every step. Adrenaline pushed through him. Unless she behaved that way whenever anyone came by to pick up or deliver something, her actions could very well inspire suspicion.

Rather than drop the box onto the garage floor, Slade carried it directly to the van and deposited it into the open back bay. He annotated the bar code number onto the clipboard's document, which he would sign and leave a copy with Mia when the task was complete.

She hovered at the garage door, waiting for the next trip.

"Is it necessary for you to follow me back and forth each trip?" he asked softly as he passed her on his way back inside.

"Yes." She moved up beside him. "That's part of my job."

He couldn't argue with that.

This time, instead of leading him through the kitchen, she made a path through the family room and formal dining area. Slade took his time following her, mentally noting the windows and doors as well as the main security panel near the front entrance.

Mia drew up short and squeaked at the office door.

One of the members of Gordon's security was scrutinizing the boxes.

"Can I help you?" she asked when she'd regained her wits.

Caution nudged Slade. This was not a part of routine procedure, otherwise Mia wouldn't have reacted in such a surprised manner. He hoped not, anyway. His internal alert rose to the next level.

"I recall you listing five boxes," the man with the wireless communications device decorating his right ear commented. He straightened from the stack and studied Mia with a measuring gaze.

Uh-oh. Slade glanced at his clipboard. "Is there a problem?" He met the other man's eyes. "I have a schedule to keep."

Mia moved into the office, pausing across the boxes from the man in the dark suit. "There were five boxes, but Mr. Gordon opted to send a number of his personal notes along with the case files. I was unable to fit the additions into the five boxes I'd packed. I'm sure if you call him he'll tell you as much, Mr. Terrell."

Slade worked at looking bored and

impatient. If Mia was lying she did a damned good job of sounding frustrated and slighted that her work had come under question.

Terrell looked over the boxes once more. "This one—" he tapped the next box on the stack "—seems to be the latest addition to the inventory." He leveled a look at Mia that could only be described as dangerous. "I'm sure you won't mind opening it so that I may inspect it and then resealing it if all is as it should be."

"This is ludicrous." Mia stamped over to the desk and scrambled through the drawers until she'd located a box cutter. "I will inform Mr. Gordon about this incident." She all but pushed Terrell aside and efficiently slid the blade along the taped seams.

"That won't be necessary, Ms. Dawson," Terrell challenged. "I'll inform him myself."

Mia stepped back and let the man sift through the contents of the box. She rolled her eyes twice before he'd finished flipping through file folders.

He closed the flaps on the box. "Everything looks to be in order."

Without a word in response, she stormed back to the desk, put the box cutter away and returned with shipping tape and a marker. When she'd secured the flaps once more, she wrote the bar code along the newly taped seam. Shifting her attention to Slade, she said, "Carry on, please."

For the rest of the trips to the van, Terrell trailed after Slade, which prevented any new free maneuvering through the downstairs portion of the house.

Gordon and his security personnel were either ultrasuspicious by nature or suspected Mia Dawson of some infraction.

Not good for Slade and the task ahead, either way.

He needed to leave a monitoring device on the main downstairs security panel. Not going to happen now. Unless he could trust her to do it.

When he'd reached the van for the last time, he placed the box inside and closed the rear doors. He annotated the final number on the pickup order, signed it and passed the clipboard to Mia. Additionally, he included the tiny device. "You'll need to look over the list I've made and ensure that all is in order. If so, you can sign my original."

She blinked, her fingers icy where they touched his. For one seemingly eternal second, she simply stared at Slade. Then she accepted the clipboard and the tiny round stick-on patch that was practically invisible.

Nodding as she read over each line, she completed her review and lifted her gaze to Slade's. The fear in those aquamarine eyes shook him hard.

"Where do I need to sign?"

He pointed to the appropriate line. "Right there will be fine."

When she leaned closer to scrawl her name across the line, Slade was careful to keep his face down. He murmured, "Put the patch on the main security panel downstairs. It's vital to the next step."

"There you go." She returned the clipboard and pen. He slipped her copy free and passed it to her. She immediately took a step back. "Thank you for coming on such short notice. I believe that's everything."

Picking up the files hadn't been on today's agenda, but Mia had worked it into the schedule to give Slade an avenue into the house.

"No problem." For a moment Slade hated to turn his back on her. She looked scared. Not good. But any unnecessary talk could create a domino effect of trouble. Her background hadn't indicated she'd ever been involved in any underhanded activity, much less anything illegal. Most likely this was a natural reaction.

One she needed to get in check.

He climbed behind the steering wheel and drove away, pausing only to wait for the gate to open.

After surveying both directions, right then left, he pulled out onto the deserted street.

Despite the cold, sweat beaded on his forehead like dew. He couldn't complete the next phase of the plan without Mia Dawson's assistance. But unless she got her act together, she would be more of a stumbling block than an asset.

He hoped like hell she pulled herself together between now and later tonight.

Otherwise—

Slade's gaze locked onto the rearview

mirror. A police cruiser pulled from a side street and moved up behind him.

"Damn it."

If she'd broken and Terrell had already called for police backup…surely Cook County couldn't have reacted so quickly. That didn't seem possible. But this was a high-class neighborhood.

Just drive. Slade held his breath as the traffic light turned green and he accelerated forward. The cruiser did the same.

A glance in the rearview mirror told him the cop behind the wheel was speaking to someone via his radio or cell phone.

Damn it!

Careful to keep his speed beneath the posted limit, Slade continued forward.

His fingers itched to put through a call to Ian…just in case.

If the blue lights came on, that was exactly what he would do.

Blue lights throbbed in the mirror.

"Oh, hell."

Slade prepared to pull to the curb.

The cruiser shifted into the left lane and barreled around Slade's borrowed van, blue lights pulsing and sirens blaring.

The relief that surged through Slade left his hands trembling.

That was too close.

Too damned close.

He glanced at the time. Three more hours until Mia got off work for the day. He hoped she could hold it together that long. As nervous as she'd appeared moments ago, he wasn't convinced she could go through with her part of the plan without falling apart or breaking under the slightest pressure.

Still, the aspect that bothered him the most with this whole scenario was her motivation.

What did she have to gain by cooperating with what could only be labeled a criminal activity? No matter what Lucas had said to her, she, of all people, would be fully aware of the risk involved.

Yet, she'd lurched her way through phase one, it appeared.

Maybe he was being overly suspicious. Lucas, as well as Ian, could be acutely convincing.

It was entirely possible that the woman just wanted to do the right thing.

Slade stifled the urge to laugh out loud at that concept. What the hell was the bottom-line "right thing" in all this?

Kidnapping and coercion were crimes any way one looked at them.

But no one involved had a choice.

The fifteen members of the Colby Agency being held hostage would die one by one if certain steps weren't taken.

Slade hoped like hell that a way to rescue everyone inside would be found before it was too late.

For Gordon.

And the Colby Agency.

Chapter Seven

Inside the Colby Agency, 2:15 p.m.

Victoria's head lolled forward. She jerked it upright. She didn't know how long she'd been tied up in the walk-in coat closet next to the lounge. Hours, she was reasonably certain.

She'd been left standing with her wrists secured to the metal rod above her shoulders. The coats had been shoved aside but the familiar scents of cologne and perfume were comforting to some degree. For a moment she closed her eyes and inhaled deeply, letting the familiar smells draw her away from this ugly reality.

Was there anything she could have done differently this morning? Could she have been more watchful…better prepared for an attack?

Victoria opened her eyes and owned the answer to those questions. No. She—they—had done all within their power to protect the agency.

Now she had to protect her staff… and herself.

At some point she had kicked off her pumps. She'd shifted her weight from side to side several times. Her legs ached and cramped. She hoped the others didn't think the worst. The last thing she wanted was for her absence to set off additional despair and desperation. She felt certain that their captors wanted just that.

Bastards.

For the first time since the siege had

taken place, her mind wandered to the possibility that she might not survive. She hoped Jim would be able to bring himself to assume control of the agency. Victoria understood that he loved his Equalizers shop, but his father had hoped that his son would grow up and take over the agency. As did she. Destiny had tossed a stumbling block into their path when Jim had only been seven years old. He'd been abducted and had suffered horrible and inhumane treatment for the better part of twenty years. It was an absolute miracle that he had been able to shake all those horrific years of physical abuse and mental conditioning to hate and to kill. He'd achieved a place so very close to normal at this point…she didn't want this to set him back.

She'd come so near to giving up hope on finding him…but she had found him. And now her family was whole again. Surely fate would not allow their reunion to be so very short-lived.

Victoria had to survive. Her son and granddaughter needed her. This agency needed her.

A trembling smile slid across her lips. Lucas needed her. She loved him so very much. For years after her first husband's death, she had been convinced she could never love anyone the way she had loved James.

But she had been wrong.

She loved Lucas with every fiber of her being. There was no question, no hesitation, not the slightest uncertainty. He completed her, just as James, Jim's father, had all those years ago.

Nor had she ever felt concerned that James would resent what she and Lucas shared. He, above all others, would have wanted her to share her life with a man he himself trusted like a brother. James would want nothing less for her than pure happiness.

And to live.

Determination solidified inside her. She would survive, by God. Whoever had set this turmoil in motion, she would not allow his vendetta to destroy her or her world.

The closet door opened.

Victoria's gaze locked with familiar gray eyes. The man in charge. She had learned to recognize him by those steel-gray eyes, and the lingering inflection that marked his voice.

"I think you've been in here long enough," he announced. He reached into his pocket and produced a knife. The blade hissed as it slid from the shaft in the handle. Victoria refused to show even the slightest hint of fear.

Glee glittering in his eyes, he cut one binding then the other. Her arms dropped. She staggered, caught herself against the door frame. Sensation rushed back into her limp arms, reminding her that they'd gone numb hours ago.

"You have a command performance, Victoria," he told her as he hustled her out of the closet.

She didn't bother asking what he meant. No need. She would know soon enough.

As hard as she tried, she stumbled a number of times on the way to her office. Inside that familiar territory, one of the man's henchmen held a video camera. So that was the kind of command performance he meant.

He intended to send Lucas and the others a message of some sort. Nothing original about that.

"Have a seat."

Victoria looked from the man who'd ushered her here to the comfortable leather executive chair behind her desk. She considered asking him what he had in mind, but she doubted he would explain himself. Arguing or delaying would only draw retribution. She was already suffering the effects of the rough treatment and mental abuse of the day so far.

Cooperation, she reminded herself as she followed his instruction. They all had to cooperate until another option presented itself.

"You're going to send a message to your husband and the others," her captor explained. "It's very simple. They are to keep in mind how precarious your situation is. You and the others are safe for now. But there can be no mistakes or your little family in there will die first. You'll watch them go one at a time."

Victoria met his vile gaze. "Anything else?"

He shook his head. "Just be sure to make your plea believable. We don't want anyone screwing up."

Victoria squared her shoulders as the man with the video camera focused in on her. She lifted her chin and stared directly into the lens.

"And—" he pressed a button "—ready."

"Lucas, Jim—" her voice quavered even as she fought to keep it steady "—we have a few injuries but everyone is safe for now. There are seven men heavily armed and as long—"

The man in charge lunged across Victoria's desk. Files and the framed photo of her family flew in different directions. He slammed the back of his hand across her cheek. The skull-rattling sting sent her head flying back. She grunted. She clamped her lips together to prevent any other outward reaction. She blinked back the burn of tears. The coppery taste in her mouth warned that he'd split her lip. She would not give him the satisfaction of tears.

He pulled back, cleared his throat for emphasis. "Let's try that again. This time leave out the number of men."

Victoria swiped her mouth with the back of her hand to clear the blood. Steadying herself, she stared into the camera lens and started again. "Lucas, Jim, despite a few injuries, we're holding up as well as can be expected under the circumstances. You must cooperate to the fullest extent if you want to ensure there is no loss of life. I beseech you to do all within your power to meet the demands you've been given." She paused a moment to swallow back the lump in her throat. "I am dictating using reasons entirely self-supplied. These are my wishes and mine alone, though at least half my staff is in heavy agreement."

"Got it." The cameraman looked to his boss for additional instructions.

"Edit it," the other man ordered, "and

we'll send it to her loving husband." He glared at Victoria.

She didn't flinch or even blink. Let him send it. She'd gotten her message across. The phrase "dictating using reasons entirely self-supplied" would signal them that she'd been coerced into the statement. Her final plea let them know that there were at least seven men, all heavily armed.

Whatever these bastards hoped to accomplish with their barbaric tactics, she had done her part to inform those struggling to devise a plan to retake the Colby Agency. There was little she could do now except attempt to keep the rest of her staff safe and cooperative.

It was the only way to stay alive until help arrived or until they could hatch a plan of action from right here inside the Colby Agency.

One that didn't include anyone dying.

The muzzle of a weapon abruptly bored into her temple.

Her breath caught. Victoria stalled. Didn't so much as breathe.

"Now, Victoria," the evil man who appeared to be in charge murmured, "let's see how successful you can be at keeping your staff alive. The first one who attempts a takeover dies."

Chapter Eight

Gordon compound, 5:15 p.m.

Mia picked up her purse and reached for her coat. All she had to do was make it to the door and out the gate.

Then she was home free.

She steadied herself, checked her shaking hands. *Focus. Be calm.* Drawing attention at this point would ruin everything.

She'd gotten the files she needed. The ones Gordon had asked her to shred. He'd claimed they were nothing more than duplicates. But Mia had taken the time to review each one and compare it with the so-called original documents.

The select group of files had been altered to agree with the outcome of certain trials. The true originals—the ones he'd asked her to shred—had reflected various witness reports and suppressed evidence that might have greatly affected the outcome of those trials. And no lack of personal, handwritten notes. Particularly the ones that pertained to her cousin's case. The one Gordon had fixed right under her nose.

But now she had him.

A smile stretched across her lips. Her shoulders reared back in triumph.

For nearly a year before her cousin's appearance at trial, she had suspected that Gordon was dirty. Now she had proof. Maybe not enough to convict him of anything that would get him life behind bars, but certainly enough to raise pointed questions and perhaps get him a nice little stint in one of the better prisons. He wasn't getting away with this. If she had her way, he would lose the big book deal. And that would only be the beginning. His name would be splashed all over the media outlets. His reputation, professionally and personally, would be ruined. And her cousin would get this life back.

Still, having Gordon end up in jail with a few of the folks he'd put there was her ultimate goal.

Then justice would take care of itself.

Ultimately she understood that without a search warrant, anything she took from his office was inadmissible in court. However, because she had included them with the official D.A.'s office files, she was reasonably sure that little loophole was taken care of.

She'd accomplished all the items on Gordon's cleanup and reorganization list.

Any working files were now a part of

the official files of the D.A. office. He hadn't kept a single page. But then he'd already made notes on all cases he intended to refer to in his memoir. The high-profile cases. All except three—those three he couldn't refer to because he'd ensured the evidence was presented in a way that indicated police tampering or other technicalities that allowed for a hung jury or a failure to present sufficient evidence for trial. Those were the ones she'd duplicated.

She had him.

All she had to do now was get out of here….

"Ms. Dawson."

Mia stopped halfway across the kitchen as Mr. Terrell's voice echoed around her.

Schooling her victorious expression, she turned around slowly and met his expectant gaze. "Yes?"

"Mr. Gordon would like to see you in his office."

Her heart lunged into her throat. *Stop. Stay calm.* "I don't have much time." She shifted the purse strap on her shoulder. "I have a doctor's appointment." Good excuse. Surely he wouldn't keep her from something as important as that.

Two seconds, then four ticked off.

"I'm certain Mr. Gordon won't take up much of your time."

Terrell stood there waiting, his arms carefully positioned at his sides. But she knew that beneath that silk jacket he wore a very big weapon in a shoulder holster. He would use it if the need arose. She suspected that he wouldn't think twice about ending the life of someone as insignificant as her, in his opinion.

"Sure." She surrendered to the inevitable and followed the head of security back to Gordon's office. *He couldn't know anything.* She silently chanted that mantra over and over.

Gordon waited behind his desk. Mia hadn't realized he'd returned. She'd only just left this office about ninety seconds ago.

"Please." Gordon gestured to the chair directly in front of his desk. "Have a seat, Mia."

She glanced at Terrell, who loitered in the doorway, then took the seat as directed.

"I have an appointment, Mr. Gordon."

Gordon clasped his hands in front of his face as if he intended to pray. But she suddenly knew better.

The only person who needed to pray was her.

"I'm very disappointed in you, Mia."

Don't let him see the truth! Ignore the accusing gaze and the disappointment lining his craggy brow.

"I'm sorry." She looked from him to Terrell and back. "I don't understand."

Gordon signaled to Terrell, who stepped aside. One of the other security thugs, wearing yet another silk suit that cost more than she earned in a month, entered the office carrying one of the six boxes Convoy had driven away more than two hours ago. Fear coiled around her throat.

She was so screwed.

"I'm not certain why you thought it necessary to include the duplicates I asked you to shred, but—" he directed her attention to the box now sitting on the corner of his desk "—you did nonetheless."

Defeat sucked at her bones. She'd been so careful. She'd tucked the files into the second of the six boxes. One Terrell would never have thought to rummage through. She'd made sure nothing important was in the sixth box, the one he'd questioned her about earlier.

"I must have misunderstood," she offered, feigning innocence. "Didn't you want everything packed up?"

Gordon eyed her for a long moment. She resisted the impulse to squirm. He wasn't a large man. Five-eight or -nine perhaps. Thin and lean. His hair was thinning and gray. The thick lens of his eyeglasses made his pale blue eyes appear far too large. Yet he had been one of the most powerful and influential men in Chicago for nearly a decade.

But he was a sleaze.

"Perhaps that's the case," he allowed. "Still, it seems quite strange to me that the documents I asked you to shred would end up misfiled in the boxes being transferred to permanent storage. You've never made a mistake like that before. That one of the cases involved your cousin can't be coincidence."

Panic tried to choke her. She'd been so careful—no one had known Terry

Campbell was her cousin. She would have been taken off the case. For the good it had done her to be a part of that circus act.

Take the offensive. "Are you accusing me of something, Mr. Gordon?"

He flattened his palms together and pressed his fingers to his lips. "I'm not certain."

Terrell stepped toward the desk.

Mia held her breath.

He opened the flaps of the box and reached inside for the manila folder in which she'd deposited the three files in question.

"Imagine my surprise," Gordon said as he accepted the file, "when Mr. Terrell opened this box and found *these*."

Go for broke. "I must have mixed that file up with the others." She nodded to the folder. "Notice that the only items it contains are the ones I was supposed to shred. I'm certain I packed it by mistake." She turned the plea up in her eyes. "Honestly, your papers were in quite a mess, Mr. Gordon, and I've been distracted about my future with the new D.A." She shrugged. "I'm really sorry about making such a ridiculous mistake. As far as my so-called cousin is concerned, we've been estranged for years. He doesn't exist as far as I'm concerned."

Please let that excuse satisfy him.

"Just a mistake," Gordon echoed, his tone as well as his expression skeptical.

She adopted a look of confusion. "What else would it be?" She glanced at Mr. Terrell once more. "I don't understand why you're making such a big deal of this."

That too-large gaze narrowed behind the magnifying lens. "If Mr. Terrell hadn't noticed that you didn't use the shredder, we might not have had the foresight to discover this *mistake*."

Damn. She hadn't thought of that. He'd said the last as if he didn't believe it for a second despite her Academy Award—winning performance.

She leaned forward. "I can assure you, Mr. Gordon," she urged, "this was just a careless mistake. After two years as your personal assistant, I would hope you know my work ethic better than that. This sort of thing has never happened before."

Mia held her breath again. Prayed her plea would divert his suspicion.

She had watched her every move. Every call. Every step. She'd spoken to no one and had carefully duplicated only information, written or oral, to use in building her case. Nothing was ever done at her condo. Instead, she drove to the library or to an Internet café to do her work. Everything she suspected, everything she had witnessed or heard, had been documented using an alias and on a Web site that could not in a million years be linked to her.

"We've been watching you for some time, Mia," Gordon went on. "Noticing your frequent early arrival or how you stayed late to finish up a task that was clearly completed. We noted how you observed my comings and goings. How you looked over my personal calendar each day. I can't prove what you were up to in a court of law, so to speak, but I do know when someone's building a case. And you—" he smiled triumphantly "—have been amassing evidence. No matter that you have the unmitigated gall to sit there and swear that it was all just a mistake."

Terrell approached her chair, placed one hand on the back behind her head, the other on the chair arm to her right, then leaned in close. "This will go much easier and far more quickly if you simply tell us what you were up to and with whom you were working."

She pushed back the clawing fear,

stared first at the man glaring down at her and then across the desk at Gordon. "I don't know what the hell you're talking about, but I do know when I'm being harassed. I will not stand for this, sir."

Gordon nodded, held a hand up to his man. Terrell immediately backed off. "I had a feeling you'd plead innocence."

How the hell could he know? She'd been so damned careful! "This is unbelievable." She stood. "Mr. Gordon, I don't fully understand what you're accusing me of, but I am both insulted and appalled."

"That was the answer I anticipated," he confessed. "That leaves me one choice."

Mia resisted the near overpowering impulse to run for the door.

"You're fired, Mia," he announced. "Leave your security badge and go. Your work at Cook County District Attorney's office is finished as well. Your severance pay will cover the weeks remaining in January. If I have my way, you will not work in this city again."

"But I—"

"Save it," Gordon warned, his face twisted with fury. "I know you've been up to something. I just can't prove what that something is. But I will not tolerate disloyalty on any level."

She shook her head. "Mr. Gordon—"

"This way, Ms. Dawson." Terrell gestured to the door. "We don't want to have to do this by force. Mr. Gordon suggested calling the police earlier, but I assured him that you would go quietly."

More than a little afraid to turn her vulnerable side to either man, she went for broke, spun around and headed for the door.

She was back at square one. She knew plenty about Gordon's underhanded deeds, but she now had not one single piece of tangible evidence. Those case files would be shredded within minutes of her departure.

And her cousin's chances of getting his life back were vanishing right before her eyes.

Through the family room and kitchen, out the garage door, she didn't slow or speak to Terrell en route. She hated when men like him used their size and lethal training to intimidate. She hated even worse that somehow her behavior had given away her plans.

She reached into her purse to fish out her car keys.

"Your key is already in the ignition."

Mia stared at the man she had despised from the day she'd met him, then she understood. "You searched my car."

"Any vehicle that comes on the property is subject to search."

The key to her condo was on that ring

as well. "And my home? Did you search that, too?" The idea that this bastard or some of his henchmen might have touched her things made her want to slap him.

Terrell smiled. "Good day, Ms. Dawson."

Furious at herself as much as at the two men who'd played her, she jerked the car door open and tossed her purse inside. She twisted the key in the ignition—only after the fact did she consider that something could have been tampered with. Her brakes. The car could have exploded.

Okay, calm down. She'd evidently watched too many movies.

No matter that she'd had all the solid evidence she'd obtained over the past year pulled like the proverbial rug beneath her feet. She still had the knowledge stored in her head and she still had Convoy.

Let the Colby Agency kidnap Gordon and turn him over to one of the many jerks he'd screwed.

Then she would have the last laugh.

She backed her hybrid up and pulled toward the gate.

Funny, she felt more relaxed and determined than she had in a very long time. That, she suddenly realized, was the mark of a truly good strategist.

Always have a backup plan.

This one, she had to admit, sort of fell into her lap, but a good plan was a good plan. Didn't matter where it came from.

Gordon would get his tonight.

Chapter Nine

*Command Center, Maggie's Coffee
House, 5:49 p.m.*

Ian, Lucas and Jim viewed the video of
Victoria a third time. Each time the knife
in Jim's chest twisted viciously, amping
up the agony. Jim wanted to kill whom-
ever was responsible for this. But first he
wanted them to pay with slow, thorough
torture.

In more than six years he hadn't
wanted to kill like this. But right now it
was a throbbing compulsion in his veins.

He would not continue to stand by and

allow his mother and her staff to be abused this way.

He simply couldn't.

They had gotten the message that Victoria had made the video under duress. That the plea was not one of her own volition was also crystal clear, but many other things were far too apparent.

The swelling in Victoria's cheek warned that she had suffered at the hands of these bastards. The stiffness of her posture spoke of the pain she felt, physically as well as mentally.

They couldn't sit back and allow this to continue.

Something had to be done.

Soon.

"We have to make a move." Jim looked from Ian to Lucas. "We can't wait for permission and allow this to continue."

The argument wasn't new. They'd gone back and forth about this all day. Ian and Lucas wanted to wait, to quietly meet the demand and then make a move. Jim couldn't wait any longer. The idea of what Victoria had suffered already was killing him bit by bit.

"No one wants to end this more than I do, Jim. But until we have Gordon or a better entry strategy," Lucas argued patiently, "there is nothing else we can do without taking unnecessary risks."

Jim turned his back on Lucas and on the monitor where the video had played out its agonizing scene. There was no getting through to Lucas. With all his years of experience in just this sort of situation, he should know better than anyone else that waiting would only increase the likelihood that someone would die. They needed to move now.

"Jim," Ian offered wearily, "your people are doing all within their power to narrow down a way inside the building without alerting the hostiles to our presence. Slade is working with Mia to gain access to Gordon when the time is right. Any other measures we opt to take at this point will carry grave risks to the very people we're attempting to protect."

Yeah, yeah. He'd heard all that before from both Ian and Lucas. He turned to face Ian. "I will not stand back and let this play out any longer. We've already established that as her son, I have the final say in the matter. Though I will continue to take your suggestions under advisement, we will proceed under my orders from this moment forward."

That same argument had been played out earlier that morning and again around noon. There was nothing further on the matter to discuss. Whatever it took to get that concept through the heads of all present, Jim was more than prepared to undertake.

"Jim!"

His attention swung to the man who'd shouted his name. Ben Steele pointed to the monitor at his workstation. "I've managed to access the security cameras inside the agency. They've been disabled so I can't retrieve any real-time images, but I can extract a number from earlier this morning before the cameras were shut down along with everything else inside."

Jim, followed by Lucas and Ian, moved to stand behind Steele. "Let's see what you've got." Jim clenched his jaw in preparation for the images.

"Victoria was right," Steele said, "there are approximately seven men inside. There could be more but I have verified visuals on seven."

Jim's mother had indicated in her message that half her staff was in heavy agreement, which, as best they could determine, translated to there being seven or more hostiles on site, all heavily armed. All present understood that whatever Victoria decided was fine by her staff, so the phrasing had to mean something else. It was an easy leap to the assessment they'd made.

The images Steele had extracted included one or two from each camera stationed inside the suite of offices. Jim flinched as the frozen scenes moved in front of his eyes one after the other. First Victoria, then Merri and Nicole… Simon—all were roughed up, then forced to the main conference room. As were numerous others as they were gathered from the exit stairwells and various hiding places in their offices. Faces were bruised and bloody.

But it was the fear in his mother's eyes that really got to Jim.

He turned to the men on either side of him—first Lucas, then Ian. "If we don't do something soon, someone will die. Mark my words." When Ian would have presented some other logic, Jim headed him off. "Those people, your coworkers—your wife—have been and will be plotting an escape scenario. You know this as well as I do. If we don't strike before they get the chance to launch an escape attempt, one or more will die for their efforts. Examples will be set."

Ian didn't argue this time. He understood that Jim was correct. Lucas kept any disagreements to himself as well. Their silence spoke volumes about the desperation level in the room. It had topped out.

Jim then drove home his point just to make sure neither man wavered in the hours to come. "What're you going to tell your children if Nicole is the one who initiates an escape plan? Ultimately sacrificing her life?"

The pallor that settled into place on Ian's face gave his answer. He didn't want to stand back and allow that to happen.

"Victoria is already resisting," Jim

said to Lucas. "You know she will do all within her power to set an escape plan or a takeover into motion. She will not continue to sit back and let the hours pass or the injustices to her staff continue uninhibited. This—" he gestured to the monitor "—passive attitude you've witnessed won't last much longer. When Victoria has had enough, she'll strike back. We're running out of time, gentlemen. Are we going to sit back and let this play out or are we going to act?"

"Building security is questioning the continued lockdown," Ian said, defeat in his tone. "I don't know how much longer we can prevent the authorities from being involved."

"What the hell are the two of you thinking?" Lucas demanded, fury searing away the emotion Jim had seen in his eyes only moments ago.

Startled by his vehemence, Jim's

control slipped. "Obviously I'm the only one who *is* thinking."

"What you're doing is hastening the deaths of one or more of the people inside," Lucas snapped. "Didn't either of you listen to what Victoria said? We are to do all within our power to meet the demand given. She isn't going to allow some rash maneuver to go down any more than she's going to commit one herself. She will ensure her people don't take any unnecessary risks."

"You can't possibly agree with doing nothing," Jim protested, allowing everyone in the room to respond to the challenge he'd just thrown on the table.

"We aren't doing *nothing,*" Lucas argued fiercely. "We're doing all within our power to find a way in without detection and we're working on giving these bastards what they want, if only temporarily. That's our job. Our only job, for now."

"Perhaps you're the one who doesn't know Victoria as well as you think," Jim argued.

Lucas went toe to toe with him. "I was there for your mother all those years when you were gone. When your father was murdered. I—" he pounded a fist into his chest "—was the one who held her hand and promised she would survive the agony. Victoria will survive this and I will see that she does. We will proceed with caution when the time is right. Anything that happens prior to that will be over my dead body."

For a time Jim could not respond. Fury blocked his ability to speak. As it slowly drained away, he had to confess that Lucas had told the truth. If anyone in this room knew Victoria…he did.

More waiting.

Jim acquiesced to Lucas's decision because it was what his mother would want.

For the first time in his life, Jim hated himself for not calling Victoria "Mother" months ago.

He'd allowed that one sore spot to fester for too long. Victoria was his mother and she deserved that title. He deeply regretted that he had not allowed her to know that he loved her on that level.

The past was not her fault. What happened to him as a child was not a result of her lack of skill as a mother. He would not let these bastards prevent him from having the opportunity to tell her just how much he appreciated all she had done before his abduction, since they had been reunited, and everything in between.

No one was going to take that away from him.

His wife, Tasha, had learned just before Christmas that she was pregnant again. He wanted to share that birth as he had his first child's with his mother.

Ian took an audible breath. "There's something Nicole and I haven't shared with anyone just yet."

Jim turned his attention to the man Victoria—his mother—trusted so completely. Ian had been with her longer than anyone else on staff. Lucas trusted him implicitly as well. Jim had overstepped his bounds.

Another first for Jim Colby. He was wrong and he wasn't about to pretend otherwise.

"Over the weekend, Nicole learned that she's expecting our third child." The hint of a smile that lingered on Ian's lips looked haunting against the agony chiseled into the planes and angles of his face. The misery had taken its toll. "It's a bit of a surprise, but we're both pleased. We had decided to wait a few weeks before we passed on the news to everyone else."

"Congratulations, Ian," Lucas offered, giving Ian a pat on the back. "Victoria will be thrilled to hear this news. When this is over, we'll celebrate."

The image where Nicole had been pushed to the floor was even more disturbing to Jim now. If that were Tasha…

He turned to his people, Ben Steele and Leland Rockford, two of his most skilled Equalizers, and said, "Find a way in. We have to move soon." He looked back to Ian and Lucas. "We will neutralize this situation before anyone else is hurt or worse," he assured the men who were as much a part of his family as his own mother. "Whatever it takes."

Ian nodded, his dark eyes uncharacteristically bright. "Whatever it takes."

Lucas looked from one man to the next and repeated that mantra. "Whatever it takes."

Chapter Ten

Outside the Gordon compound,
6:05 p.m.

Something was very wrong. Mia should have departed the property by now.

Slade reached for his binoculars yet again, but it was pointless. From his position on a side street, he couldn't see anything beyond that twelve-foot wall.

"Damn."

He couldn't call her cell phone. He couldn't do one damned thing except wait for a move from inside the compound.

The small transmitting device he'd

asked her to place on the first-floor security panel would jam the control frequency when activated. Until the device was turned on it remained undetectable. When the moment came that entry to the house was needed, a split second of interruption in the frequency would be all that was required. By the time any remaining security personnel recognized that something had gone wrong, it would be too late to prevent the intrusion. Worked like a charm every time.

Slade was prepared to make the necessary extraction but there was a lot he needed to know about Gordon's movements and an extraction right now would render her assistance impotent to a great degree. Mia would brief him on all he needed to know as soon as she was out of the compound safely.

He glanced at his wristwatch once more—6:12 p.m.

His head moved from side to side with worry.

If she'd broken and given away the plan… Gordon would no doubt call the police. Then…hell, unless Jim, Ian and Lucas came up with a better plan…

Slade didn't want to think about that. Too many lives depended upon this going down exactly as planned.

The gate started its slow swing inward. Slade sat up straighter. Adrenaline lit in his veins. The idea that she was late evoked a whole series of hard questions. Had she been questioned or had she suddenly decided she couldn't be a part of this?

Maybe she'd simply had to work some overtime.

When she'd driven past his position, he waited another five seconds, then pulled out onto the street. He followed her to the rendezvous point—a convenience store well beyond the residential area Gordon called home.

He guided his truck into the slot next to Mia's hybrid. She stared forward, not bothering even a brief glance in his direction.

Bad sign.

Slade swung out of his truck and walked around to the passenger side of her compact sedan. The door was unlocked. He opened it and dropped into the passenger seat.

"What happened?" He couldn't resist stealing a look behind them to see if the police showed up to haul him in for questioning. Conspiracy to commit kidnapping was a crime. Not one taken lightly. Particularly when the target was rich and famous.

"I was fired."

She didn't look at him as she made this startling statement.

He'd expected a lot of things to come out of her pretty mouth but that wasn't one of them. "Fired? On what grounds?"

Her face turned to his and that blue gaze, the color of the deepest sea, bored into his. "He…said I had failed to live up to the expectations of the position since he left office and that the new D.A. had his own personal assistant."

She looked away before the explanation was out of her mouth. Slade's gaze narrowed. Why would she lie to him about something as seemingly inconsequential under the circumstances as this? He was no trained expert at spotting untruths but an expert was hardly needed to see right through the garbage she'd just passed off as the gospel.

"What about the promotion you'd hoped for?" Something about this was all wrong. The coincidence that this "firing" occurred on the same day that she'd been approached by the Colby Agency for assistance wasn't lost on him.

"There won't be any promotion." She

dropped her head back against the seat. "I'm out. End of story. It's over."

There was little he could do about that, though he regretted she'd lost her job. Too much of that going around these days. "Were you able to put the jamming device into place on the main access panel on the first floor?" As painful as this was for her, he had a job to do. Each step was crucial.

She nodded. "Exactly as you instructed."

Another thought occurred to him. "They took away your access to the property, didn't they?" Without her badge, getting through the gate wouldn't exactly be a piece of cake. That was a huge step backward even with the device in place. Climbing the wall would only work if they knew exactly where the motion sensors were placed.

Slade hoped the others could come up with a plan to infiltrate the Colby Agency

building without the necessity of dragging Gordon into this. The man behind the siege was clearly out for vengeance. The Colby Agency wasn't in the habit of succumbing to terrorists and those thugs could only be called exactly that.

Mia started the car and turned to face Slade. "There's something I need to show you."

He tapped the button on the key to his truck to secure the doors. "All right." His instincts started humming once more. Mia Dawson was about to give him something relevant to the task before him. A part of him hoped like hell this would prove some sort of turning point, leverage that would work to the advantage of the agency's reputation. Bending the law was one thing, but breaking it was entirely another.

She pulled out of the parking lot and drove to the nearest discount home improvement store. When she'd maneuvered into one of the parking slots, she grabbed her purse and got out of the car.

Slade followed her across the big lot. He didn't ask questions. She didn't offer any explanations. Inside, she snagged a shopping cart and headed down the main aisle as if she had a specific destination in mind.

As the main aisle intersected the extra wide middle aisle, she paused to meet his gaze. "I want you to go into the men's room and wait for me there."

"The men's room?" Had he heard her right?

She selected a light fixture from an end cap. "Yes. I'll be there in three minutes."

"Whatever you say." Slade strolled across the massive warehouse, pausing occasionally to survey the sale items on an end cap just to fit in. When he reached the restrooms, he entered the men's room and scoped out the place. Five stalls, all empty. Now this scenario…was just this side of weird. He leaned against the corner of the first stall and waited for her arrival.

At the end of three minutes, just as she'd scheduled, the door opened and she waltzed inside.

Her expectant look had him assuring her, "All clear. What's this about?"

She chewed on her bottom lip a moment. "I haven't been completely honest with you."

He'd picked up on that. "In what way?"

Reaching up, she ran her fingers through that long, silky black hair. "There's no way I would have even heard you out this morning. What you were suggesting would have seemed ludicrous…except…"

The silence lagged. "Except?" he prompted when she failed to continue.

He needed to know what the hell was going on here.

"For the last year I've been watching Gordon a little closer than I used to. I recognized some inconsistencies in a few of his cases and I felt compelled to look into the situation for—" she shrugged "—you know, little discrepancies. The kind that can tilt a case the other way."

He didn't want to spook her by suggesting that they have a conference call with Ian and the others. Taking her to the command center was too risky, particularly since she'd been fired. Gordon could have someone on his security team watching her. The situation at the Colby Agency was precarious enough without adding any additional layers of trouble.

Another snag Slade would have to deal with in the coming hours.

"Did you find anything to back up your suspicions?" Seemed a safe enough question to ask at this point in the conversation.

She licked the lush lip she'd been abusing with her teeth. "Yes. I…I found evidence that Gordon had sold out in three cases in the past fifteen months. There were a couple of others, but some proved more difficult to connect the dots, so I focused on the ones I could decipher more readily."

"Is this why you were fired today?"

Her head moved up and down, affirming his suggestion. "That's also why I was willing to go along with your plan. Gordon has been selling out victims when the price or the outcome was to his advantage. He isn't the pillar of the community everyone believes him to be. I had hoped that I'd be able to pull together enough evidence to blow his cover or at least to topple his self-righteous empire. But his chief of security, Terrell, noticed my indiscretion on the number of boxed files to be moved to permanent storage."

Slade had taken those boxes to the storage facility himself. "The boxes I picked up and delivered to the county facility?"

She nodded. "Terrell apparently went through them before they were shipped out. Both he and Gordon suspected what I'd done."

"Made copies of certain documents?" Seemed like the most logical step. Documentation of wrongdoing would be the easiest evidence to prosecute. After some serious time in a D.A.'s office, she would certainly know this was a good way to at least cover her own back.

"Yes. Handwritten notes on certain aspects of cases. Altered official documents. Notes," she went on, "that were never introduced into the prosecution's game plan. Twice defendants were never bound over to grand jury because of a lack of tangible evidence. Both times the outcome should have been vastly different. In one case, the lack of those very notes ensured that the case was lost by a jury vote. I know because I was a part of that investigation."

"What made you think the evidence you compiled would be admissible in court? You took it without a search warrant." That was something else she had to know without any coaching from him. A technicality could ruin the best case.

She made a little sound. Under other circumstances it might have been a laugh. "I knew what I was doing." She tapped her right temple. "I have lots to tell stored right here. I just wanted a little hard evidence, you know. I figured if I shipped it to the storage facility and then went to the D.A. with what I know, this would lead to where I'd sent the files—"

"He could issue a search warrant for

Gordon's files." Slade got the whole picture now. "Could've worked. Definitely."

"No kidding." She dropped her head back and blew out a disgusted breath. "Now…" She lifted her head and stared into Slade's eyes for a bit before continuing. "Now I don't know."

The door opened. Slade's attention swung to the man who'd entered.

"Sorry," Mia said quickly. She backed toward the door, moving wide around the newcomer. "I'm—" she gestured vaguely to the wall that separated the two bathrooms "—supposed to be next door."

Slade started after her. At the other man's confused look, he mumbled, "We're arguing…she wasn't paying attention."

Mia was already shoving the cart down that center aisle once more. Desperation and defeat were fueling her confusion. Slade hustled to catch up with her.

"What do we do now?" she asked without looking at him.

He fell into step with her purposeful stride. "That's the big question. According to the last call I received from Ian, there's still no workable plan for getting into the building. Which leaves us with—"

"Me." Her gaze met his. "Just so you know, Mr. Convoy," she said as she pushed the shopping cart back into the long line of carts near the front entrance, "I'm ready to do whatever it takes to see Gordon go down. Legal or not."

"We'll pick up my truck and go to my place so we can talk." They walked side by side out one of the exits and to her car. "I'll put through a call to Ian and get an update on the situation there."

She moved around to the driver's side while he waited at the front passenger door. After reaching for her door, she hesitated, stared at him across the roof of the vehicle. "I don't know you very well, Mr. Convoy. Why can't we go to my place?"

He took the remark with an acknowledging nod. "Is it safe to talk openly at your place?"

She blinked, considered his question a moment. "Maybe not. We'll go to your place."

Slade hesitated then, his hand on the door handle. She was disgusted, angry, hungry for revenge. If he let her do this…she could go down with the rest of them.

He pushed away the second thoughts. Their options were limited.

She was their one ace in the hole.

Slade Convoy's home, Joliet, 7:49 p.m.

MIA STEPPED INTO the little bungalow Slade called home. He even had a yard with a little fence, though it was too dark to get the full effect. She wondered if that meant he had a dog.

She hadn't had a dog since she was a kid back home on the farm in Iowa. A long, long time ago.

"It's not much," he offered humbly. "A work in progress mainly."

She gingerly stepped around what looked like a huge carpet shampooer. The floors were hardwood, as far as she could see. Maybe he had rugs.

"Floor sander," he explained as he pushed the shampooer look-alike out of the way. "I'm going to refinish these floors one of these days. I actually had plans to start today."

She turned all the way around in the small living room. Pale yellow walls, probably the previous owner's selection. Convoy didn't look like a yellow kind of guy. But she liked it. Felt warm. God knew it was as cold as hell outside tonight.

"If you're hungry, I could order something to be delivered."

Code for: I don't keep food in the house.

"I'm okay for now." She dragged off her coat and tossed it onto the cluttered leather sofa. The furniture looked fairly new and of incredibly good quality. "Can I see the rest?"

"Make yourself at home." He peeled off his coat and dropped it next to hers.

Two bedrooms, one bath and a neat but compact kitchen. She parted the blinds and peered out the back door. A dim light barely cut through the damp gloom. There was no moonlight and no stars in the sky. The perfect creepy atmosphere for her present predicament.

She wandered back into the living room, where Convoy was deep into a call on his cell. After trying but failing in her efforts not to listen, she realized he was ordering pizza. The old reliable.

A guy couldn't go wrong with ordering pepperoni and cheese.

"Fifteen minutes," he told her when he ended the call. "I think I have beer and…water."

"Either'll be fine." She shoved aside a newspaper and collapsed on the sofa. God, she was exhausted.

He hurried to declutter the sofa and matching chair.

"Nice furniture." If he'd picked out the furnishings, he had excellent taste.

"My sister showed up one afternoon and had this stuff delivered." He laughed. "All I had to do was pay for it."

"Then your sister has good taste."

He lowered into the chair across the coffee table from her. "I spoke to Ian en route."

He'd mentioned that he intended to make that call. "What's the plan?" Gordon wasn't getting away with what he'd done to her cousin or to her. Fear of legal retribution wasn't going to stop her. Not now. He'd royally screwed over too many people. She could blame her actions on temporary insanity.

"I'm assuming Gordon has cameras inside the house just as he does outside."

She nodded. The man was a security freak. Not that she blamed him, considering what she'd discovered he had been up to.

"Ian suggested that you play the part of uncooperative informant. That way—" Convoy leaned fully back in the chair "—you won't get charged when this is done. If Gordon and the police believe you were coerced into leading me inside, it'll be far better for you."

She couldn't argue with that, but she wasn't so sure she wanted to be eliminated. Plea bargains were given all the time. She could trade her inside knowledge on Gordon for a lighter sentence.

Besides, she was proud of the fact that she was doing the right thing.

"Maybe I don't want to appear unwilling." She might as well put that card on the table. It would give her great pleasure for Gordon to know she'd gotten him in the end.

The private investigator rested his forearms on his wide-spread knees and clasped his hands between them. "I'm not sure you're looking at this with a rational view. You're angry right now, that's no place to make a decision from."

"I know what I'm saying and doing, Mr. Convoy." She wasn't a kid. She was a grown, educated woman. If helping him round up Gordon and turn him over to one of his enemies would save more than a dozen lives, she was all for it. He'd had it coming for a very long time.

"And if he ends up dead? Or someone else does, our people or one or more of the thugs inside? Are you prepared to stand charged for those actions?"

Murder One would be hard to beat. There was no denying the premeditation. A plan was not only useful, it was absolutely necessary.

"But you said you had a strategy to help ensure his safety." She recalled that Ian Michaels or Lucas Camp, maybe both, said Gordon wouldn't be sent in without a backup team in place.

"Definitely, but when weapons are involved there is no sure plan. You need to bear in mind what's best for your future."

She pushed to her feet. "I need to use your powder room."

"If you need anything, let me know," he called behind her.

Inside the cramped bathroom, she closed and locked the door. She turned to the mirror over the sink. She stared long and hard at her reflection. Dark circles traced the area beneath her eyes.

"What're you doing?"

She looked tired and way older than her twenty-nine years. Convoy had explained that two of the women being held hostage were pregnant. Several were mothers. Most of the men were fathers.

Mia couldn't let those people die.

Considering what Gordon had done, he deserved what was coming to him. She's spent half a decade estranged from her cousin—the whole family had. The man had gone from one scam to another for most of his adult life. Then he'd grown a backbone and a conscience and decided to do the right thing by testifying against his superior at the savings and loan. Terry had sat in that courtroom and exposed the lending institution's underhanded deeds—including taking government bail-outs when it was undeserved. Gordon had seen to it that his professional reputation was ruined, ultimately ensuring that his career in pretty much anything was over. And Terry's superior had been acquitted.

Mia couldn't let Gordon get away with this. Lawyers and cops bent the law every day. This was no different.

Except someone could die.

Shaking off the disturbing thought, she attended to her needs. As she was washing her hands, she couldn't help but notice the masculine scent of his soap. Smelled nice. Sexy.

Like him.

Mia promptly dismissed the crazy thoughts. She'd let down her cousin and lost her job today. Gotten caught trying to take down a criminal, who just happened to be her boss. Latching on to the basics, like sexual attraction, was a normal reaction.

But that was one situation she intended to stay far away from. She'd never been too good at the whole relationship thing. Her work always got in the way.

Moments later, the smell of pizza filtered through the house. Her stomach rumbled.

About time her appetite showed up once more.

Convoy had spread the open box and a couple of beers on the coffee table.

"Smells great." She didn't wait for an invitation. She grabbed a slice and sank her teeth into the thick pie, then moaned her satisfaction.

He did the same, only without the sound effects. By the time they'd reached for their second slices, they'd relaxed.

"Shortly after midnight," she announced before tearing off another juicy bite with her teeth.

"For moving in on Gordon?"

"He's always in bed by midnight and his sole security guard is pretty much covered up with keeping the house and property secure."

"I'll confirm this with Ian and then we'll get some sleep. It's going to be a long night."

She would bet the next slice of pizza that he was the kind of guy who never slept when there was a job to be done.

"I'll keep you safe," he promised. "You have my word on that. Whatever happens."

Funny, she wasn't worried about that in the slightest.

Convoy made his call to his superior then polished off another slice of pizza.

Mia thought about calling her parents. She was the only child. If anything happened to her they would be devastated. But if she called, one or both would instantly recognize that something was wrong.

It was best not to leak the information to anyone. The fewer who knew, the better.

If she died…she wondered what Gordon, assuming he didn't end up dead as well, would release to the media about her.

She'd known soon enough how this would play out.

Assuming any of them survived.

11:35 p.m.

SLADE MOVED SILENTLY to the door of his bedroom. He hated to disturb Mia but it was almost time. He'd urged her to get an hour or so of shut-eye before midnight. She hadn't wanted to, but he'd eventually talked her into taking his bed and at least trying to sleep.

When he'd confirmed that she'd drifted off into dreamland, he'd made a call to Ian. Slade's instincts were nagging at him. Mia Dawson's professional résumé didn't match her story. She was a strict professional. Loyal and dedicated to a fault. The idea that Gordon was a lowlife wasn't nearly enough motive to send her over the legal line she was about to catapult across. Every instinct he possessed screamed that this was *personal*.

Very personal.

But how? She'd sworn she and Gordon weren't intimately involved. Not a single hint that she'd lied existed. That kind of thing was almost impossible to keep under wraps when a high-profile political figure was involved. That meant it had to be something else…something related to a family member or a friend. Something big and ugly.

Ian had found it. One Terry Campbell, first cousin to Mia Dawson. Campbell had decided to rat out his superior at the independently owned and operated Windy City Savings & Loan. Only it had backfired. The defense had come up with enough dirt to completely discredit him as a reliable witness. Since

Campbell's word was all the D.A.'s office had when key pieces of evidence were thrown out on technicalities, the case had gone south. Campbell had lost his job. His gold-digger wife had walked out since he no longer had anything to offer. The man was already estranged from his family, including Mia. He'd attempted suicide twice in the past four months.

Now there was a strong motivation.

Slade crossed the room in sock feet, his movements silent. He leaned down and touched her shoulder. "Mia?"

She bolted upright, her arms coming up in front of her in a defensive manner. The strangled scream sent regret searing through his bones. She had no real comprehension of just how badly this could end.

"Hey, it's me," he urged as he sat down on the edge of the bed. "Time to get ready to go." The light that filtered in from the hall allowed him to see how her eyes had rounded. She was scared to death.

She sucked in a breath, held it, probably to slow her too-rapid respiration. "Sorry." She scrubbed her hands over her face and pushed all that long, dark hair back. "I was having a bad dream."

"About your cousin?" No need to beat around the bush. This mission was far too important to play games.

"I…" She blinked. "I don't know what you mean."

So she was gong to play it that way, was she? "I know what happened to Terry Campbell. I understand why you want to have your revenge, but this isn't about your cousin or revenge. This is about keeping people alive. People I care about." He leaned over and switched on the bedside lamp. She squinted. "If staying focused is going to be a problem—"

"No." She shook her head adamantly. "I can do this. It's the right thing to do."

He searched those gorgeous blue eyes. "You sure about that? Blood is thicker than water. I don't want you going commando on me and trying to mete out justice yourself."

"That's what my cousin said," she offered, her expression determined.

"That you shouldn't settle a score with Gordon?" Slade was confused now. Ian's research had indicated the cousin was estranged from the rest of the family.

"That it was the right thing to do." She drew in another of those deep breaths, the movement luring his gaze to her chest. "He contacted me only days before he turned himself over to the feds. The whole case was supposed to be played out in federal court. But Gordon somehow managed to get the case shifted to his jurisdiction. If Terry's boss had been proven guilty, the feds would have taken the next step. But Gordon made sure that didn't happen. I had my suspicions but I didn't have anything concrete so I kept my mouth shut." She pulled her knees to her chest and hugged them. "Terry lost everything. And I let it happen. No one in the family will believe anything he says. He's lied so much." She searched Slade's eyes then. "If I don't fix this, he'll just keep trying to end everything and…"

She fell silent. A fat tear rolled down her cheek. Slade couldn't help himself, he had to reach up and swipe it away with the pad of his thumb. Her skin felt so soft. Her lips quivered and he wanted desperately to make that fear go away.

"The Colby Agency will help you set the record straight." He traced the line of her jaw, cupped that softness in his hand. It felt good to touch her. "I'll help you." He stretched his lips into a reassuring smile. "You have my word."

"I wanted to fix this…to be the one who made it right since I allowed it to happen. But today I realized I couldn't do it alone." She leaned her cheek into his palm. "It's all so surreal. I don't know what to trust anymore."

"You can trust me." He leaned forward, placed a chaste kiss on her other cheek. "We should—"

She reached her arms around his neck, pulled his mouth to hers. He knew he should resist. They didn't have time…he didn't have the right…but he couldn't draw away. She tasted of fear and desperation and sweet, soft woman. Her fingers threaded into his hair and a sound of approval swelled in his throat.

At last she dragged her lips from his, rested her forehead against his chin. "Sorry," she muttered. "I just needed to know how you kissed." She looked up at him then. "I've never met a man like you. You're…" A shrug of uncertainty lifted her shoulders. "You're different from the guys I usually run in to."

He fingered a length of her silky hair. "Later," he promised, "when this is over, we'll see where *this* goes."

Right now, they had to go kidnap a former district attorney.

Chapter Eleven

Gordon compound,
Tuesday, January 21, 12:15 a.m.

She could smell his scent on her skin.

Mia felt completely idiotic noticing, but after half an hour sitting in his truck— in the dark—alone with him, there was little else to notice. The kiss…she had to have been out of her mind. But she'd needed to feel something real.

Focus, Mia! This is not the time for selfish needs.

He said they were in wait mode. Ian had to call and confirm the orders to move in.

Admittedly, she would be happy when this part was over.

Never in her life had she done anything illegal. Well, maybe she'd stolen a pen or two from work. Come to think of it, the stapler in her home office had come from work. But not any criminal activity for real.

She turned to Slade Convoy. And to commit the act with a total stranger was a little off the charts for anyone, especially her. Her parents wouldn't understand. Neither would her few work friends. Personal friends were too few to mention. Who had time? She worked long hours…and, secretly, she'd opted to go back to law school last term. One class at a time would be slow. But she would get it done.

Sounded like a good hobby in prison. Lots of prisoners got their educations while behind bars. She could certainly do the same. The idea sent a shudder through her. Or maybe it was the man next to her. She'd never been kissed like that. *Focus!*

They had parked at the corner of the neighboring property just across the street. Though they hadn't waited in this spot for long, she was surprised the police hadn't cruised by and checked them out. The street remained totally empty. The quiet somehow surrounded them like a protective blanket.

Convoy—Slade, he'd insisted she call him Slade, or maybe she'd said it first—reached into his jacket pocket and pulled out his cell phone. The call he'd been expecting, she supposed. Now maybe they would do something besides sit in the dark and wait.

Adrenaline rushed through her body, sending goose bumps spilling across her skin. She gazed out over Gordon's property. If it was time, she was ready. Ready to see his face when he was in the same vulnerable position his victims had experienced. To see him lose everything the way Terry had.

Jerk.

"Understood," Slade said before closing his phone. He turned to her. "We've been cleared to proceed with entering the house and obtaining Gordon's cooperation."

Who was he kidding? Gordon wasn't going to cooperate with anything that didn't benefit him somehow.

At that instant the anticipation bottomed out and fear howled through her veins.

She was really going to do this.

Slade opened his door and got out. She told herself to move, but nothing happened. *Just get out.* Her hand jerked, that same fear coursing along her limbs as she reached for the door handle.

Then she was out of the truck, both feet on the ground. The night air was cold. She shivered. It was January after all. The silence felt deafening. The ambient lighting pooling along the property wall looked too bright.

How could she and Slade possibly hope to get inside? She no longer had her security badge. The codes had surely been changed.

"This way," Slade murmured as he shrugged a backpack into place.

She followed him in the shadows of the tree-lined street until they reached the corner where two properties met. Then they crossed the street. Her heart thumped harder and harder. If anyone looked out their window, drove by or was for some reason out for a late-night stroll, there would be no place for them to hide.

The neighbor's shrubbery lined the exterior of Gordon's stark wall on the west side. Slade moved between the shrubbery and the wall.

When she was close enough, he said, "You said the motion detectors monitoring the other side of the wall were located approximately twenty feet apart."

She nodded. "I remember distinctly Gordon bringing the blueprints for the fancy system into the office. He was extraordinarily pleased with himself about the property and the new security system he'd contracted to be installed. That's what happens when you get a seven-figure book deal."

Slade motioned to the wall. "If I clear the other side without triggering the alarm, you follow the same route."

She nodded her understanding. *She had to be out of her mind.* The phrase kept echoing in her head. This was the first of many laws she would be breaking. She might as well get used to it.

He pulled a square object from his

backpack. She couldn't tell exactly what it was. About the size of a small cosmetic case. He aimed the sort of square package and something shot from it. Hit the wall. He checked to see that the line extending to the top of the wall was steady and secure. He reached out and took her hand. She trembled. He placed her hand against the line. "Feel that?"

"Yes," she whispered.

"If you grab hold and squeeze it'll take you up with no sweat."

Her head made that acknowledging up-and-down motion. This wasn't possible. Couldn't be real. She had to be dreaming. Okay, Mia, pull it together.

Then something incredible happened. He held on to the line and it lifted him to the top of the wall. He reached up with one hand, threw one leg up onto the ledge and pulled himself up. When he was safely astride the ledge, the line from the boxlike mechanism slid effort-lessly back down to where she waited.

He'd told her to follow the same route if no alarms sounded.

Truly crazy. She licked her lips. Grabbed on to the line with both hands. Squeezed. Her breath evacuated her lungs as her body was propelled upward. Just as abruptly the line jerked to a stop.

Slade didn't speak but he reached down to give her a hand up onto the ledge. Her head swam as she settled her bottom onto the broad limestone ledge. The grounds of the property looked eerie in the darkness…or maybe from this position. Had she ever been afraid of heights? Maybe, but she'd never been in a position to find out.

He tinkered with the line and box, settling it so that it would drop down the other side—the inside of the wall. He gestured for her to pay attention. She moistened her lips and watched his every move. When he grabbed securely on to the line, it dropped to the ground, taking him with it. He landed firmly on his feet but not enough so to throw off his balance. Immediately, he flattened against the wall and waited.

For her. Mia took a breath and followed the steps she'd watched him take. She swallowed back a scream as the line reeled her downward. Somehow going down felt faster than going up. Her feet hit the ground, forcing her knees to bend a little.

He pressed his face to her hair. "You said the guard on duty makes a round of the exterior perimeter at half past the hour, correct?"

She nodded, resisting the urge to tremble at the feel of his mouth against her ear.

"As soon as we see him move beyond our position, we're heading for the house."

She understood, let him see her comprehension.

They left the line in place and carefully moved across the yard, using the islands of shrubbery and architecture as cover. Thank God for her vigilant observation of her surroundings. She'd been helping Gordon at the house for several months. Each day when she'd taken her afternoon walk on the grounds, she'd made a mental note of where everything was, including the security sensors.

Not once during that time had she ever considered that she would need to know those things in order to break in to Gordon's house.

Second thoughts twisted in her stomach.

The security guard suddenly appeared around the front corner of the house, flashlight bobbing with each step. Mia held her breath and watched him pass. When he'd done so, Slade went down on one knee next to a group of shrubs only a few feet from the patio. He dropped his backpack to the ground and rummaged through it for the next gadget he would need, she assumed.

One thing was certain, she'd never met anyone like him. Her life was full of lawyer types and court clerks. Not a single one of them would know where to even begin to accomplish a goal like this one.

They didn't teach stuff like this in law school.

He got back to his feet and made a noiseless path to the French doors beyond the patio that led into the family room. She'd already assured him there were no motion sensors around the exterior doors. The remaining motion sensors were inside. Each window and door was outfitted with a magnetic strip to set off the alarm if one was opened while the system was in active mode.

Holding his hands out palms up, she mimicked the move. He placed a small cloth bag in one hand, then rolled it open like a travel cosmetic carrier. Holding a miniature flashlight with his teeth, he knelt down in front of the door and picked the lock with instruments that looked very much like what a dentist would use.

Mia's job was to watch for the return of the guard. She craned her neck to survey both ends of the house. *Just let them get inside without being spotted.*

When he'd returned the instruments to the bag, rerolled it and placed it back in his backpack, he withdrew something resembling a remote control. One click in the direction of the living room and he waited, watching the series of lights on the handheld device.

When all went to green, he grabbed the handle and opened the French door. She followed him inside. Her body was thankful for the warmth but her mind was reeling with denial and fear.

More of that thick silence waited inside.

After closing the door, he said, "We don't have much time. Go over the locations of the interior motion sensors with me."

"At the bottom of the stairs near the front of the house, as well as the second staircase in the kitchen. I can't remember seeing any others."

"Let's go, then. We need to get up the stairs before the system's connection resumes or the guard comes back inside."

She rushed up the stairs behind him, the thick tread runner cushioning the noise their shoes might have made otherwise. If she was ever rich she wouldn't have a runner on her stairs. When an intruder struck, she wanted to hear him coming.

They had cleared the staircase. Relief made her legs quiver. From here, she led the way.

The distinct chime told them the guard had come back inside and deactivated the motion sensors. He would check the interior of the house next, move from room to room and ensure all was as it should be.

Slade had a plan for that, too.

They moved to the guest room nearest Gordon's suite and took up their positions.

The guard typically needed ten minutes to make his rounds downstairs, then moved to the upstairs.

Stretched out like a cat on the guest bed, Mia tried to listen for his approach over the blood roaring in her ears.

The beam of his flashlight moved over the room before she heard him at the door.

She closed her eyes, giving the appearance of sleep. The glow of the flashlight lit on her face. A softly muttered curse echoed in the room. The guard started toward the bed.

Slade stepped out from behind the door and grabbed him from behind, closing one hand over his mouth as he disabled him. Mia hugged herself as she pushed up into a sitting position. She was extremely pleased that Slade didn't really hurt the guy. But his movements had looked…well…brutal.

Nothing at all like his kiss.

"The duct tape," Slade muttered.

She scooted off the bed and dug the duct tape from the pack still hanging on his back.

When he'd carefully secured the man, including his mouth, Slade removed his cell phone, security badge and keys. Grabbing his flashlight from the floor, the two of them relocated the still unconscious guard to the walk-in closet. This was one she hadn't met. Nothing about him looked familiar.

Time to go for Gordon.

Mia stayed close behind Slade's tall frame as they moved down the dimly lit corridor to the double doors that led into Gordon's suite.

She had started to relax. So far, it wasn't so bad. A little scary when one considered the risk. Breaking and entering. Assault with duct tape and some kind of kung-fu-style training. But Gordon was living on borrowed time, whether he realized it or not.

Slade reached for the doors. Mia held her breath. No light shone from beneath the doors. He was most likely asleep by now.

Still, if he was watching the television with the sound muted, or reading the newspaper using nothing but a subtle side-table light.

She wrung her hands together.

Just stop.

They were very close to attaining their goal.

Soon this part of the operation would be over.

Slade opened the doors wide and stumbled back two steps.

Mia blinked, told herself she had to be seeing things.

"Who're you?"

A scantily clad woman stood directly in front of them, just inside the doors leading to Gordon's suite.

"I'm calling security!" she shouted.

Chapter Twelve

Maggie's, Command Center, 1:03 a.m.

Ian Michaels hesitated in his pacing. Convoy should have contacted him by this time.

"Nothing yet?"

Ian met Lucas's worried gaze and shook his head.

"Something's wrong." Jim stepped away from the workstations where his men were getting closer to an entry strategy with every passing moment.

Unfortunately, Ian agreed with Jim's assessment. Convoy should have called in by now. If he had failed to attain his goal of infiltrating the Gordon compound, they needed to know sooner than later.

Even more disturbing, if the police had been involved, the whole operation would be blown.

"We have no choice but to wait for some indication from Convoy or that location." Ian didn't have to clarify what the latter meant. If the police were summoned, they would know very soon.

"I don't understand why that bastard doesn't answer the phone." Jim stalked back over to the front window and peered through the darkness at the building across the street.

The man in charge of the takeover inside the Colby Agency had refused additional contact. He'd given his demand and he had no intention of discussing matters until he had what he wanted.

Gordon.

Until Gordon was in their possession, they had no leverage.

This was the first time in all his years at the Colby Agency that Ian had given the order to break the law. No matter what Lucas or Jim said, this was his responsibility. He would be the one to face charges if worse came to worst. That was as it should be.

As long as Nicole and the others were safe, he did not care what happened to him. Ensuring the safe return of his wife and the others was all that mattered.

Lucas kept checking his cell phone. Ian was certain he hoped Victoria would have an opportunity to get a call through. Or that his former superior would call with the news that one or more members of his old unit, the Specialists, were back in the country and could help with this nightmare.

Ian closed his eyes. He was very tired. He'd called hours ago and spoken to his kids. A neighbor was taking care of the children for him.

Jim had touched based with his wife, Tasha, several times. She wanted to be here, to help. But their daughter, Jamie, needed her at home.

"They're at it again."

At Jim's remark, Ian moved to the window. He watched the lobby a moment before seeing the flashlight beams scan the area. The group was vigilant about security. He had to give them that. But that reality only made the concept of getting inside without drawing their attention even more impossible.

Ben Steele and the other man from Jim's shop had deconstructed the building via electronic technology. Each new entry point revealed led to a dead end. The building's designers had worked diligently to ensure there was no way to infiltrate the structure.

One of the architects was deceased. The other had been diagnosed with advanced Alzheimer's last year. That left the trial-and-error method Steele and his associate had been conducting for hours nonstop.

Ian's cell vibrated. His heart all but stopped. He looked at the screen, didn't recognize the number.

Jim and Lucas moved in closer. No one wanted this to be the authorities.

"Michaels." Ian told himself to breathe.

"Daddy, I can't sleep."

Relief flooded Ian. "Natalie, what are you doing up at this hour?"

Jim and Lucas backed off, their expressions bearing out the combination of relief and anxiety they both felt.

"Miss Mary said I could call you since I couldn't sleep."

"Nat," Ian coaxed cautiously, "whose phone are you using?" He didn't recognize the number.

"Miss Mary needs a new phone," his daughter explained. "She's using her mother's cell phone."

Thank God. Thank God.

"Where's your brother," Ian had the presence of mind to ask. "Is he sleeping?"

"Yep. He always sleeps."

"I'm sure if you go back to bed, close your eyes and try really hard," Ian suggested, "you'll be able to get to sleep."

"Daddy?"

"Yes, darling?" Ian's chest squeezed.

"When is Mommy coming home?"

Ian collapsed in the nearest chair. He didn't have the heart to respond to his daughter's question.

He didn't know the answer.

Chapter Thirteen

Gordon compound, 1:59 a.m.

Mia pressed a length of duct tape on the woman's mouth, but that didn't stop her from squeaking and groaning. Mia shook her head. "I'll go see where Gordon is hiding."

"Be careful," Slade called after her before turning his full attention to their unexpected guest.

Who the hell was this woman? Mia hadn't mentioned that Gordon entertained women friends.

Slade lifted the woman into his arms.

Her ankles and wrists were bound and still she struggled against him like a frantic fish. He carried her into the guest room and stashed her in the walk-in closet with the still unconscious guard. Since she'd been dressed for bed, her cell phone hadn't been on her person. Leaving any sort of communication device in the closet with them would be plain dumb.

On second thought along those lines, he secured the woman's wrists to her ankles to prevent her from trying any escape maneuvers. The fear in her eyes tugged at his insides. Like the guard, she was an innocent victim in this disaster. Slade hated like hell to do this to her but he couldn't take any chances. Telling her to go home and forget all she'd seen wouldn't cut it.

"Don't worry," he assured her, "you'll be fine."

Unable to bear the overflowing tears

at this point, he backed away, exited the closet and closed the door. After a quick survey of the room, he scooted a chest of drawers in front of the door. He didn't want either of them coming up with any harebrained ideas about escaping and causing trouble anytime soon.

Now for Gordon.

Slade took a deep breath and headed back into the corridor. As soon as his brain had assimilated what his eyes saw, he stopped dead in his tracks.

Mia waited in the middle of the broad upstairs hall, her hands held high above her head.

Gordon, clad only in silk pajama pants, stood in the open doorway to his room. The revolver in his hand was aimed at Mia. A combination of fear and adrenaline exploded in Slade's muscles. Something else Mia apparently hadn't known about.

The gun.

Two realizations penetrated the shock strangling his mind at the same time.

Gordon wasn't wearing his glasses.

And he didn't look at ease with the weapon in his hand.

Both of those factors could work in Slade's favor.

"Put your hands up," he shouted at Slade.

Slade took his time raising his hands. "Take it easy, Gordon. You don't want to shoot anyone."

"Ha!" he barked. "You're both intruders." He waved the barrel at Mia. "Especially you." The accusation came out a snarl. "I'm calling the police."

Slade braced for a move. The man didn't have a house phone or a cell phone in his hand. He'd have to get to a phone to use one.

"You're a criminal," Mia shouted right back at him. "I'm going to prove it. I want to see you pay for what you've done rather than living in the lap of luxury."

Slade took advantage of the distraction to move a few steps closer to Gordon's position. If Mia could keep him focused on his former cases, maybe…

"What're you doing?" The weapon's business end swung in Slade's direction. "Stop right there."

"You're not going to get away with what you've done," Mia warned, determined not to let her fury go. "Whatever I have to do, I'm going to prove it."

Gordon glared at her with utter derision. "No one's going to believe a word you say. I fired you for incompetence. Anything you say now will be considered sour grapes or plain old revenge. You're a fool if you believe you can trump up some sort of ridiculous charges and have a snowball's chance in hell of making them stick. You're a fool, period."

"No." The word was out of Slade's mouth before his brain had had time to clamp his jaw shut.

Gordon glared at him once more. "What the hell do you know? You're just brawn for hire."

"Actually," Slade told him as he took yet another step in the man's direction, "I'm from the Colby Agency and everything she says is true. You have committed atrocities against your office and the citizens you represent. For those you will pay."

"Stop right there!" The gun in Gordon's hand shook. "I will shoot."

Maybe he would. Slade had come unarmed due to the nature of the job. If the police arrived, no member of the Colby Agency was going to be found armed on the premises after breaking and entering. Too risky.

Besides, he'd had no reason to suspect Gordon kept a gun in the house.

Disabling the security guard had been simple. Slade hadn't expected Gordon to brandish a weapon. Mia had never known him to be anything but anti-gun. He sure as hell didn't have a registered license for a weapon. The agency had checked. Slade had to neutralize this situation quickly.

No one was supposed to die.

"No one will get hurt, Mr. Gordon," Slade argued, "if you just put down the weapon."

Gordon shook his head. "Nothing doing. That bitch isn't ruining all I've worked for."

"You did the ruining yourself," Mia countered. "Someone has to stop you."

Mia needed to back off just a little. She was pushing Gordon too hard. Slade's cell vibrated a second time. Ian was concerned... Slade was supposed to have checked in by now.

"First," Slade said to the man, drawing

his attention back to him, "she's not a bitch. She's a very smart lady who saw through a lowlife like you."

Gordon's mouth twisted with outrage. "If she's so smart, what's she doing sneaking in here like this?" He aimed another harsh glare at Mia. "Any lawyer or even law student worth her salt would know what is and isn't admissible in court. And this, my dear, is not admissible in any fashion. Whatever you came here to get, you've wasted your efforts."

"This isn't about your arrest, Mr. Gordon," Slade said, more to shock him than anything. He needed the man vulnerable. He needed to gain control of that weapon before someone got hurt. He also needed to call in and confirm that Gordon was in custody.

The minutes were ticking by.

"What are you up to?" Gordon demanded.

"Justice," Mia announced.

Gordon whipped his attention back to her. "Don't you see, Ms. Dawson, there is no real justice. Only the facsimile created by those with enough money or enough influence to determine how the story should end."

"In a few hours we'll see if your definition of justice remains the same."

"Too bad getting fired sent you over the edge, Dawson." He shook his head. "You might have made something of yourself. I don't know what you came here expecting to find or get, but, as I said, you've wasted your time."

Mia shook her head. "Not at all. We came here to get you."

Gordon charged forward.

Mia stumbled back a step.

Slade rushed between them.

The explosion of the revolver discharging shattered the silence.

GORDON HIT THE CARPETED floor with an *oomph,* Slade on top of him. The weapon bounced out of reach.

"Get the weapon!" Slade shouted.

Mia didn't go for the gun. Slade didn't have time to glance her way. He had to get Gordon subdued.

Screaming profanities, the older man squirmed and attempted to kick Slade. Slade twisted to miss the blows but didn't release his grip on the bastard.

"Duct tape," Slade called out. "Get me the duct tape!"

The duct tape suddenly appeared in front of his face. The hand holding it shook but that wasn't what seized Slade's attention. Blood trailed from beneath the coat sleeve's cuff and down Mia's pale hand.

Fear seized his chest. His gaze sought hers. She was as white as a ghost. "You okay?" he demanded, instantly taking note of the rip in the upper portion of the right sleeve of the coat she wore.

Mia nodded once, her expression frozen in one of shock.

Focus, man! "Secure his ankles while I hold him down," he ordered.

Another single nod.

Slade forced the man's hands above his head and settled his weight down the length of him in an effort to keep him as still as possible.

Don't think about the blood. She's upright and breathing. Most likely a flesh wound.

"Don't touch me!" Gordon wailed. "Don't touch me, you crazy bitch!"

"Don't move," Slade growled, ready to head-butt the fool if he didn't shut up and hold still.

"I'll get you both," Gordon threatened. "You'll see!"

Slade's jaw tightened as he crushed

downward with his full weight. "Be still," he growled.

"Got it," Mia muttered. She moved to stand near Slade's left shoulder.

He resisted the impulse to stop what he was doing and check out her arm. He pushed up onto all fours, then rolled Gordon onto his stomach. "Don't fight me," Slade warned. "You're only hurting yourself."

Whatever Gordon said was muffled by the plush carpet.

When Slade had the man's wrists pushed together, Mia dropped to her knees and wrapped the tape around once, twice, three times.

"I'll take it from here." Slade nodded toward her arm. "Take off the coat and see what kind of damage you've got."

He finished securing Gordon. If she was injured badly… He shouldn't have allowed her to leave the room to check on Gordon. This was his fault.

Damn it.

Using more force than necessary, he rolled Gordon onto his back once more and slapped a length of tape across his mouth. His struggles lessened marginally, probably from exhaustion. But Slade wasn't taking any risks. He wanted this sleazebag properly secured.

Slade got to his feet, stepped away from his prisoner and moved closer to Mia. The bullet had torn through the fabric of her coat and the blouse she wore. Red had pooled around the damaged section of the fabric now plastered to her arm.

"Take off the blouse."

Those blue eyes glimmered with fear as she reached up to do as he'd asked, her movements wooden.

"Here—" he reached out "—let me."

She didn't say a word as he loosened the blouse then peeled it away from her torso and arms. His heart rate accelerated as much from seeing the lush rise of her breasts above the satin cups of her bra as from the raw, jagged flesh where the bullet had left its piercing path. His gut tied into knots.

"Thankfully it looks as if it's nothing more than a flesh wound."

She nodded, then leaned her head to the left. "He's trying to get up!"

Slade wheeled around and with one booted foot shoved Gordon back to the floor. He snatched up the duct tape and knelt down next to Gordon. Slade rolled him onto his side and tethered his ankles to his wrists. "Try it now, old man," he challenged.

Getting back to his feet, Slade returned his attention to Mia. "Let's get that cleaned up." He reached down and grabbed Gordon by the arm. With little effort he dragged the bound man into the middle of the master bedroom.

Mia had already turned on the light in

the en suite bath. Slade made his way to where she stood before one of the sinks staring at her reflection in the well-lit, ornate mirror. She still hadn't said much and her movements and reactions were stilted at best. Not surprising. He doubted she'd ever been shot.

Slade searched until he found the items he needed. Clean washcloths, peroxide, an antibiotic ointment, gauze and tape. The gauze and tape appeared to have been around awhile, but it was still in the original packaging.

"This may hurt a little," he offered gently as he began the cleanup. "But it won't hurt for long."

A faint laugh whispered across her lips. "I seem to recall hearing that when I was seventeen and on the verge of losing my virginity." That weary blue gaze collided with his. "Next you'll tell me that it'll be more fun next time."

"Seventeen, huh?" he teased as he

cleaned the wound and rinsed with peroxide. A couple of stitches wouldn't hurt, but that wasn't happening right now. He'd been right in his assessment that it was a flesh wound. A few minutes of pressure to staunch the bleeding would help.

She winced, but remained steady. "Yep. High school sweethearts. I figured since everybody else was doing it, I might as well see what all the fuss was about."

"I'll bet you asked questions during the whole experience." He thought of all the questions she'd asked when he'd appeared at her door.

Another of those fatigued laughs. "Well, let's just say I wasn't the only one who didn't particularly enjoy it."

"That," he said, applying the ointment, "is because you were with a boy. A real man knows how to make sure his woman enjoys every moment."

She actually smiled. "I'll remember that."

Slade placed the gauze over the wound in layers in case there was more seepage, then secured it with the tape. "I could help refresh your memory whenever you like."

The silence stretched between them as he rinsed the washcloth and cleaned the rest of her arm. He held her hand under the flow of water and washed it clean as well.

When he was all done, she looked down at herself and her cheeks flushed. "What do I do about this?"

"Gordon's lady friend was wearing a negligee. Surely she has something around here."

While Slade gathered the ruined blouse and weapon, Mia slid on the lady's sweater. She flinched a couple of times, but managed the feat alone before grabbing her coat. The torn sleeve wouldn't prevent the garment from keeping her warm. The woman secured in the closet probably had a coat around here someplace, but hunting it down wasn't on the agenda at the moment. The sooner they got out of here, the better.

"You all set?" he asked.

"Yeah." She glanced at Gordon. "Let's get this done."

Slade hesitated. "You're sure this is the way you want to play this?" Gordon understood that she was a willing participant but it wasn't too late to salvage the situation as far as any other witnesses were concerned.

"Yes." She took a breath. "I'm not ashamed of what I'm doing. It has to be done."

Slade couldn't help himself. He leaned down and left another of those soft, quick kisses on her cheek. But her eyes told him that would never be enough.

"You could," she whispered, her face so very near to his, "refresh my memory of that kiss we shared earlier."

"No problem." His lips brushed hers as he spoke. A quake of pure desire vibrated through him. He let his lips cover hers completely…let himself feel the need and desire quivering in her slight body. She leaned into him, allowed him to experience her heart beating against his chest.

All they had to do was survive the next few hours and then he would show her so many pleasures…if she still wanted to explore this thing escalating between them once the adrenaline rush was over.

Chapter Fourteen

Maggie's, Command Center, 2:50 a.m.

Jim watched Ian's preparations. He would drive to the Gordon compound to check on Convoy and Dawson. There had been no contact and time was swiftly running out. It was imperative that they understand what was going on.

Nothing had been reported on the police band. Whatever was happening over there, so far the police weren't involved.

Steele pushed back his chair and turned to face Jim and the others. "I may have it."

Relief sent a twinge through Jim's chest. "How difficult will it be?"

Steele turned and tapped the screen of his computer monitor. "It won't be easy, but there's a path I believe will work for a man with the proper skills."

"That would be you," Jim remarked.

Lucas moved up behind Steele to get a look at the point of entry and path for reaching the Colby Agency's suite of offices that had been discovered.

Ian stiffened. He reached into his jacket pocket and removed his cell phone. "Michaels."

The whole room froze, all eyes glued to Ian.

"Open the back door. They're here," he said to Jim.

"What about Gordon?" Lucas asked.

Ian nodded. "They have Gordon in custody."

Jim took the stairs two and three at a time. He rushed through the kitchen to the rear entrance that opened into the alley between the buildings. After shoving the dead bolts back, Jim wrenched the door open, his heart hammering.

Gordon, mouth taped shut, hands secured, was the first face he saw. Dawson and Convoy were right behind him. Jim ushered the former district attorney inside. "Good work," he said to Convoy. "We were beginning to get worried about you."

That was when Jim noticed the blood on the woman's coat.

"What happened?"

"It's nothing," she insisted. "The bullet barely scraped the skin."

Jim's gaze locked with Convoy's. "Gordon had a weapon stashed in his nightstand."

Damn. "We'll have someone take a look at that," Jim said to Dawson.

Mia Dawson glared at him, then brushed past him and stomped up the stairs to the command center. Evidently, she wanted no special attention.

SLADE FELT CONFIDENT that having a bullet miss a vital organ by mere inches wasn't exactly how Mia had expected the confrontation with Gordon to go.

Or maybe he'd pushed too far with his suggestions...or the kiss. But she'd seemed willing enough.

Slade settled Gordon into a chair amid the buzz of the command center on the second floor.

"Rocky," Jim said to his teammate Leland Rockford, "take a look at Ms. Dawson's arm. Apparently Gordon got off a shot that grazed her."

Lucas and Ian shared a look with Slade. "Gordon had an unlicensed weapon in the table next to his bed."

Ian shook his head. Lucas let go a weary breath.

Slade's attention rested on their special guest. They were close now... but at what price?

4:00 a.m.

"WHAT THE HELL are you doing?" Gordon demanded.

Mia ignored Gordon's blustering. She glanced at the new bandage around her upper arm. She'd tried to tell the man called Rocky that she was fine—that Slade had already taken care of her—but the big guy wouldn't listen. If it hadn't been for Slade's quick reaction and that big coat she'd been wearing…it could have been so much worse.

Gordon would have killed her.

Any possible sympathy she may have cultivated for the man had died a sudden death when the hot metal grazed her flesh.

Gordon had been outfitted with bullet-proof clothing. Mia had no idea such protective wear existed. He'd refused to cooperate, prompting Ian and Slade to tug and pull and drag the protective wear as well as his slacks and shirt into place.

Mia had gotten the clothes from his closet while Slade ushered the man into the garage. Then, despite the fact that her arm had been hurting like hell—still did—she'd driven Gordon's fancy sedan across town with Gordon and Slade safely ensconced in the backseat. Slade would pick up his truck later.

"How are you coming along with that route?" Jim Colby asked one of the men seated at a computer.

"Printing it out now."

They had a little more than three and a half hours before Gordon had to be turned over to the bad guys. If this route into the building panned out, Steele, one of Jim Colby's men, the way Mia understood it, would go in and take care of the threat. Ian Michaels had briefed her and Slade on the plan. Ian had put through a call to another Colby Agency investigator. Well, not exactly a staff member, but a potential one. Penny Alexander's clearance wasn't in place yet, but she possessed certain skills that would be beneficial to this operation. Ian had decided to call her in if she could be located.

"We have a problem."

The collective attention of everyone in the room swung to the man Rocky standing at the window. Mia couldn't react for a moment. They didn't need any more bad news.

Grabbing back her courage, she joined the others at the window. Blue lights flickered and flashed. Four—no five—Chicago P.D. squad cars had descended upon the small visitor parking area in front of the building across the street.

The Colby Agency building.

"Did you hear from the security company?" Jim asked Ian.

"An hour ago," Ian assured him. "They had agreed to stand by until ten this morning."

"Somebody apparently didn't get the message," Jim said, his tone grave.

The tension that spread through the already stressful situation seemed to squeeze the oxygen out of the room.

Gordon laughed like a fool. They should have left the tape on his big mouth. "My guard must've escaped your incompetent attempt at securing him."

Slade nodded. "That's possible. I secured the guard and the woman in a guest room closet."

More of that idiotic laughter from Gordon. "Now we'll see who's the criminal," he said to Mia.

"How would he know where to send the police?" Mia argued.

Gordon's face twisted with stifled mirth. "We have your apartment wired. We heard what your friend proposed to you. We knew what you were up to, we just didn't know the when. That's why I had a gun in my nightstand." Gordon glanced around at the grim faces. "Whoever your client is, he can go to hell."

Ian moved to the stairs. "I'll see what I can do." He jerked his head toward Gordon. "You might want to put him somewhere out of the way, like in the freezer downstairs."

Jim patted the shoulder of the man at the computer. "Keep working on it. We'll take care of this situation."

Slade and Jim escorted the still manacled Gordon down the stairs and to the kitchen. He shouted most of the way, insisting that he could not be put into the freezer.

Mia wished she had the duct tape so she could shut him up again.

Since there was no walk-in freezer, the walk-in cooler had to do. Mia and Slade joined Gordon inside, to stay out of sight as much as to keep him quiet. Slade had grabbed a hand towel en route.

He pried Gordon's mouth open and shoved enough of the hand towel inside to shut him up.

It was barely lit inside the cooler and only because Slade had thought to flip the exterior switch before they were locked inside. With Gordon moaning in the corner it was damned depressing as well. Already he'd thrown a stumbling block in the works. How could she possibly hope to bring him down? The only person going down was likely her…and Slade.

"You okay?"

She met Slade's green eyes. She liked his eyes. But she was so tired. Her cousin's future hung in the balance. She had no job. Gordon would see to it that she faced legal charges. "No, I'm not okay."

Careful of her injured arm, Slade put his arm around her shoulders and pulled her to him. "We'll get this all worked out." He tipped her chin up to him then. "Trust me, will you?"

She tried to smile but her lips were too cold and too tired. "I'm trying." Truth was, she did. Was that crazy or what? She barely knew him.

He caressed her cheek with the pad of his thumb. A shimmer of warmth went through her. "I owe you dinner at least. You really hung in there."

"So did you." She liked having his arm around her. She liked him. She liked his kisses even more.

He placed a soft kiss on her forehead. It wasn't the most romantic place she'd ever been kissed, but it was by far the most romantic kiss she'd ever had the pleasure of experiencing.

"I promise we'll finish *this* later."

"Definitely." Taking yet another risk, she stood on tiptoe and brushed her lips to his. The heat that simmered through her veins made her forget all about being in a massive refrigerator. She'd made the first move once already. But he was worth the risk.

The door abruptly opened.

"The police are gone," Ian reported.

Slade and Ian ushered Gordon back to the second floor. Mia kind of floated along behind them. She didn't know how this day was going to end but she did know one thing for certain—she had something to look forward to.

Slade Convoy.

When Gordon was settled and secured to a chair once more, Ian removed the towel from his mouth and slapped a strip of tape there before he could start ranting again.

Jim suddenly let out a whoop. All gazes landed on him.

"We've got it," he explained. "Rocky has gone to bring the necessary gear and Steele is ready to go in."

"Ms. Alexander is on her way," Ian mentioned.

The two men didn't argue, but there was a shared look of mere tolerance.

Ian reached into his pocket and pulled out his cell phone. "Michaels."

Lucas, Slade, Jim and even Mia fixed their attention on him. Had something else gone wrong? Just because the police had left didn't mean they actually believed Ian's story about the ongoing gas/electrical problem in the building. He'd convinced them that Gordon's security guard was no doubt delusional.

Ian started to argue with his caller twice, then a third time. Each time he appeared to be cut off. Finally he said, "I understand."

He closed the phone and dropped it back into his pocket. "We have thirty minutes to turn over Mr. Gordon or a hostage dies."

"What?" Jim demanded.

"He moved up the timeline?" Lucas shook his head. "This is not what we agreed to."

"I can't get in there that fast," Steele said to Jim, who was looking at him hopefully. "That's an impossible deadline."

"That's the point," Ian said. "He says the arrival of the police prompted him to move up the timeline, but I'm convinced it's because we had Gordon on site and he didn't want us to have any extra time to plot a counterattack."

Mia looked from Ian to Slade. "What do we do?"

Slade held her gaze for a long moment. "We give them what they want."

Chapter Fifteen

Inside the Colby Agency, 4:30 a.m.

Victoria stirred. It was dark in the conference room. And so quiet. Her head hurt, but more than that her chest hurt. She, Nicole and Simon had managed to keep everyone calm and cooperative. But she wasn't sure how much longer that strategy would work. Her entire staff was growing more nervous by the hour.

"Victoria."

She turned her face toward Nicole's voice. The other woman moved closer as soundlessly as possible so as not to alert the guard at the door.

"Simon and I believe we have enough manpower to overtake these guys."

The whispered words struck sheer terror in Victoria's heart. "No." She shook her head to emphasize the word. "Not yet. There's still time—"

"Simon overheard them talking," Nicole interrupted. "The timeline has been moved up. Something is supposed to happen very soon. We can't just keep playing dead…or we'll all end up that way."

More of that fear trembled through Victoria. "I'll try a strategy I've been mulling over first." When Nicole would have argued, she cut her off. "That is a direct order, Nicole. I'm trusting you and Simon to keep the others safe. They are your responsibility. Is that clear?"

Nicole heaved a frustrated breath, then nodded.

The door opened and the overhead

lights beamed to life. Victoria squinted, blinked to adjust to the brightness.

The man she recognized as the bastard in charge pointed at her. "Victoria, step up here with me."

The man shackled to the chair across the room started to struggle against his bindings. He moaned pitifully. Victoria wished she could see his face. Could help him.

"We still need water," she told the leader of this unholy troop as she scrambled to her feet. Her numb legs tried to buckle under her. The guard rushed to steady her and escort her to his superior.

"That man—" Victoria indicated the man whose identity they didn't know "—needs water."

The leader grabbed her by the face and squeezed. Victoria's staff stirred. She prayed they would be very, very still. Thankfully she heard Nicole's soft voice urging the others to remain still and quiet.

"You have a special job this morning," the man in charge said to Victoria.

She blinked back the sting of tears as his fingers continued to crush her face.

"You," he went on, "have the distinct pleasure of helping me select who will die first."

"I'll go first."

Victoria's breath caught at the sound of Simon's voice.

"Well, well," the bastard gripping her said, "we have ourselves a hero."

Victoria strained to see her wonderful staff—family, really—huddled together on the floor. A moan rose in her throat as Simon Ruhl pushed to his feet.

"That's right," Simon agreed, "that's all you need, right? One hero?"

The man released Victoria's face. "Maybe. Maybe not. Depends upon how long your friends take to respond to my schedule change." He grinned at Simon. "I'm not so sure they have your best interest at heart."

Simon cautiously moved closer to the man in charge. "Let's step outside and give them some motivation."

"No." The single word wrenched from Victoria's throat. When the leader turned back to her, she said, "I am the head of the Colby Agency. I will go first."

Another of those nasty grins stretched across his face. "How sweet. We have two heroes."

"You're wrong."

Victoria's lungs seized as Nicole struggled to her feet. Victoria's head was moving from side to side, but Nicole wasn't looking at her.

"You have three heroes," Nicole announced.

This time the bastard didn't laugh.

As tears poured unimpeded from Victoria's eyes, each and every member of her staff stood, one by one, and offered to die first.

The man cut a look at Victoria, that steel-gray gaze churning with hatred.

He opened his mouth but, before he could say whatever vile remark that was poised on the tip of his tongue, his cell phone rang loudly.

Without taking his eyes off her, he snatched the phone from his waist. "It's about time," he snapped. A long pause indicated whoever had called was speaking at length. "Excellent. Don't be even a second late or—" his gaze shot to Victoria's "—your beloved Victoria will be the first to die."

Chapter Sixteen

Maggie's Command Center, 4:40 a.m.

"Jim," Lucas implored, "I will escort Gordon. There's no need for you to take that risk. Victoria would not be happy about that."

Jim stood his ground. "This discussion is over. I'm going in." Before Lucas or Ian could argue further, he asked Ben Steele, "How long before you're prepared to move in?"

Rocky had arrived just moments ago with the gear Steele would need. "I'm ready now."

"You'll need assistance," Ian argued. "Penny Alexander will be here in the next five minutes. I'd like her to go in with you. She's fully prepared to meet the necessary physical rigors."

"I don't want him to wait," Jim protested. To Steele he said, "Go."

"Jim, you're moving too hastily."

Jim sent Ian a hostile glare. "I'm not waiting any longer." He glanced at the clock on the wall. "We have less than ten minutes. One second late and Victoria dies. I won't take that risk."

Slade stepped forward. "All of you need to be here to get the backup team ready and in place. I should be the one to take Gordon in."

Gordon groaned against the tape keeping his mouth closed.

"I should do it."

Everyone turned to stare at Mia.

She took a deep breath. "I know more about what he's done than anyone else.

I've also been involved with most of the cases he has worked the past two years. I might recognize someone." She shrugged. "Learn something, maybe."

More of that annoying noise from Gordon.

"No way," Slade said. "You're staying right here."

This time Mia was the one standing her ground. "Have you bothered to look at his prosecution history to try and determine who the hell is behind this? This kind of takeover requires some serious motivation."

Lucas held up a hand. "We have. We've confirmed the whereabouts of all the players in every case he prosecuted for close to three years back…except two. We couldn't locate anyone from the Dennison case or the Thorp case. We're still working on that."

"The only family member of the victim in the Dennison case," Mia explained, "died last year. Cancer. So that's likely a dead end."

"That leaves only one," Ian said, pointing out the obvious.

"The Thorp trial," Mia said with a threatening glare at Gordon, "is one of the cases I believe Gordon screwed up. The killer went free."

"That's the one where his daughter was murdered," Ian commented, apparently remembering some headline or news report.

Mia nodded. "Mr. Thorp tried for months to raise awareness in the media and at the D.A.'s office, but he was stopped."

"Where is he now?" Slade asked, a bad, bad feeling leeching beneath his skin.

"He was jailed about three months ago on harassment charges." She glared at Gordon again. "Something else you're responsible for."

"Wait." Lucas looked around the room. "How do I know that name? Am I the only one who's heard it before?"

"The victim was actually his stepdaughter. Patricia Henshaw," Mia clarified.

"Oh, good Lord." Lucas's face paled. "That was the murder trial last summer…the one on which Victoria served as a juror."

Understanding dawned on Ian's face. "We can't take Gordon in there. It would surely be a death sentence for him."

"We can," Jim said as he walked over to the man whose hands and mouth were secured and jerked him to his feet, "and we will. There's no time to do anything else. If we don't, it's a death sentence for a lot of innocent people."

"Jim, wait." Slade stepped in front of the big guy. "This will not end well. I'm afraid I agree with Ian. It's time to call the police."

"No way. Step aside, Convoy."

Slade knew enough about Jim's past not to doubt that he would clear his path by whatever means necessary. But he couldn't let this happen. The Colby Agency's reputation was already fractured. This would push it way past merely broken.

"If you go in like this, emotionally charged, you could end up just another hostage," Slade said, throwing out one last argument. "Let me go."

Jim shot Ian a look. "Tell your man to step aside."

The minutes were ticking by too damned fast.

Ian rested his too-somber gaze on Slade. "Step aside, Convoy. We don't have any more time."

Jim Colby marched down the stairs with *their* hostage in tow.

Slade's gut twisted into knots. This could be the end…

"I don't know about the rest of you," Lucas said as he walked stiffly toward the stairs, "but I'm going out front. If anything goes wrong, I want to be as close as possible if there's any chance I can help."

Tears had started to stream down Mia's cheeks. Slade reached out and squeezed her good arm.

"Where's justice when it's needed?" she asked with a hiccupping sob.

He gave his head a little shake. "I can't say. But the Colby Agency is the one place that it still exists. Maybe, if this is Thorp, this is the only way and place he felt confident he could find it."

They walked down the stairs together.

On the sidewalk, in front of Maggie's Coffee House, Slade, Mia, Ian and Lucas stood together and watched Jim Colby walk away, walk toward the Colby Agency, where the first hostage was scheduled to die in a mere four minutes.

Victoria was to be first.

Maybe Jim was right. Maybe he was the only choice to finish this.

Chapter Seventeen

Inside the Colby Agency, 4:58 a.m.

Victoria stood before the receptionist's desk in the greeting lobby of her agency. Thankfully the rest of her staff remained in the conference room. She didn't want them to be subjected to this atrocity... particularly if things went wrong.

Her heart pounded so hard she could scarcely catch a breath. The muzzle of the handgun bored painfully into her temple. She refused to show this bastard that he continued to cause her pain. So she stood stoically, without flinching.

She would give him no satisfaction on that level. Focused, she watched and waited for the elevator doors to open.

Someone was escorting former D.A. Timothy Gordon to exchange for the release of the hostages. She wanted so desperately for all her people to be safe. She had prayed and prayed that this moment would arrive.

But not at this price.

Victoria had already made up her mind. She wasn't leaving her agency or the man, Gordon. Or the other unidentified hostage. Whatever the reasons for bringing those two men here…she would not leave either to be murdered in her stead. But she would wait until the rest of her staff was released before taking that stance. She wanted all of them out of harm's way. If they learned of her plan, they would refuse to leave.

But this was her ship and she would go down with whoever remained, good, bad or indifferent. It was her duty.

"Sixty seconds," her captor growled. He bored the muzzle more deeply into the thin flesh of her temple. "Maybe they've decided to let you all die. You are getting up there, after all."

Victoria resisted the urge to smile. Obviously this man did not know Lucas or Jim or Ian. Not one of the three would allow this to happen.

She had long taken the stance that the Colby Agency did not negotiate with terrorists. But now she'd seen that there were times when there was no other choice but to negotiate. She thanked God that this was the only time she'd been forced to be a part of a horrific decision like this.

This was a sad day for the Colby Agency.

In far too many ways to count.

The light above the elevator flashed, signaling that a car had arrived. Then the distinct ding announced that the doors would momentarily open.

Victoria held her breath. Prayed for the strength to stand firm with her decision to remain after the others were released.

"About damned time," the man with the gun snarled hatefully.

The doors slid open slowly. The first man she saw she recognized as D.A. Gordon. His mouth was taped closed and his hands were bound in front of him. Her gaze moved beyond him to identify his escort and her pulse seemed to grind to a halt.

Jim…her son…had escorted Gordon into the building. Why would he take such a risk?

Jim pushed Gordon off the car when he clearly did not want to exit. There had to be a way for Victoria to help him survive whatever was to come.

"You have what you asked for," Jim said, his voice gruff, feral. "Now release the hostages." He kept his gaze steady on the man with the gun pressed to Victoria's head. Not even for a split second did his attention deviate to her.

"Well, well," the bastard said, "the venerable Colby Agency came through after all."

"I'm waiting," Jim warned. "Let them go. All of them. Now."

The bastard gripping Victoria's arm like a vise shouted to his men. Two came running to his aid. "Take Gordon," he ordered.

"No way." Jim drew the man back against him. "You let the hostages go first and then you can have him. But not an instant before."

"How brave of you, sir," the leader mused. "I know my men searched you in the main lobby on the ground floor. You have no weapon. No cell phone. Nothing. And yet you would dare to defy my direct order."

One corner of Jim's mouth twitched

with the shadow of a smile. "And I will kill you for touching my mother."

Tears welled in Victoria's eyes. He'd called her his mother. She'd waited so long for him to feel that connection strongly enough to use the endearment. Before she could restrain them, the tears billowed over and flowed down her cheeks.

Still, Jim did not look at her. He kept that fierce glare locked on his target. Victoria wondered if the man had any idea how savage a killer her son had been in the past. Would those statistics scare him in the least? Jim had been a monster, but he'd overcome those lethal impulses. No matter, she loved him for who he was now and for who he'd always been.

The man made a sound that he likely considered a chuckle. But it was far too vile to contain any humor. "Release the hostages in the conference room," he said to his men. "Lead them down the stairs. Have one of those waiting across the street call and verify that all are accounted for."

Relief left Victoria weak. She prayed her son would look at her so she could tell him with her eyes how very much she loved him and how very much what he'd just said meant to her.

Gordon started to squirm. Jim tightened his grip on the smaller man. That was when Victoria saw the tears sliding down Gordon's cheeks as well. Dear God, how could she allow this?

Yet, she had no choice. Too many lives were at stake.

Two minutes, three, then four passed before the bastard's cell phone sounded a warning that a call was incoming. He released Victoria's arm to take the call. The weapon, however, stayed burrowed into her flesh, which held her still.

When he had confirmed that it was Ian calling, he tossed the phone to Jim. "There's your verification, tough guy."

Jim listened while Ian passed on the required information. "Very good." He closed the phone and tossed it back to its owner. "Now, release the final hostage and we're finished here."

"Now," the bastard said, echoing Jim, "this is where things get dicey. You see, I can't release Victoria. She's part of the second phase of this operation. Remember—"

"In that case, the deal is off," Jim roared, cutting him off. He reached behind him and pounded the call button with his fist. "You don't release Victoria, you don't get Gordon."

"Ah, not so hasty, Mr. Colby," the man in charge began. "If you remember the demand was twofold. One, bring Gordon. Leaving Victoria behind is part two. I opted to keep that to myself until it became necessary to tell you."

"No way." Jim glared at the man, his eyes warning that he was at the very end of his ability to maintain restraint. He would not be able to hold back his baser urges much longer.

"This is nonnegotiable." The flat statement rang in the air.

Victoria wished she could do something, anything to stop this travesty.

"We haven't called the authorities," Jim reminded him. "If that's what you're worried about, we won't until you and your men have cleared out."

"If only that were true," the leader countered. "Whether it is or not is actually inconsequential. Your mother is needed for phase two."

"It's all right, Jim," Victoria urged. "I need to stay. I can't walk—"

"No talking," the man with the gun snapped, grabbing her hair and digging the muzzle deeper into her skull.

Jim postured to make a dive around Gordon.

Victoria pleaded, "Please, Jim, just go."

Jim's gaze locked with hers. For the briefest moment she saw the misery… the unspoken feelings. He didn't want to lose her…he loved her.

Victoria smiled faintly. She told him with her eyes how very much she loved him.

"You have sixty seconds," the man in charge announced. "Release Gordon to my men and leave or she dies."

Jim's attention swung back to the man with the gun. "Release her and keep me instead."

"Won't work, fifty seconds."

Dear God, Victoria prayed, *just let my son walk away.*

Jim's gaze searched hers once more. For three endless beats she was afraid he would attempt to overtake the man with the gun…no matter that two more of his henchmen had joined him.

"Thirty-five seconds," the man roared. "You'd better make up your mind whether your mother's brains are going to be spread all over this lobby or not. I'm running out of patience."

Three, four, five seconds elapsed. Victoria held on to hope that her son would leave safely.

Jim pushed Gordon forward, turned his back and entered the waiting elevator car. Then he faced her one last time.

Victoria would remember those moments before the door closed for whatever remained of her life. Her son loved her deeply. He'd shown her with his eyes.

"Take him to the conference room," the brute said to his men. Then he dragged Victoria over to the window and crushed her face against it. "I want you to watch your son walk away. It's the last time you'll ever see him."

Victoria's heart filled with pride as Jim came into view, exiting the building. His stride was long and strong as he crossed the parking area and then the street. Lucas and the others waited for him on the other side. Her staff, her family, hugged, held each other close. She didn't have to see the tears to know they wept. For each other. For her.

For the day the Colby Agency ceased to be what it once was.

Chapter Eighteen

5:50 a.m.

Lucas's heart dropped to the sidewalk.

Jim was crossing the street *alone*.

Lucas walked out to meet him, his leg giving him hell. "Where's Victoria?"

Jim's chin jutted upward. "They wouldn't release her. I tried to exchange myself for her but they refused. She refused as well."

A lone tear trekked down the savage man's face. His pain was as real as anyone's here, including Lucas's.

Lucas nodded. "You did all you could.

Victoria is a strong woman. She'll figure a way out of this. We have to believe she will triumph."

Ian moved over to join them, Nicole held close at his side. He repeated Lucas's question. Before anyone could answer, his cell chirped. He pulled it quickly from his pocket. "Michaels."

Silence fell over all those gathered.

Ian drew the phone from his ear and set it to speakerphone. "You're on speaker," he said tightly.

The man still holding Victoria, no doubt.

"Enjoy your freedom!" the bastard exclaimed. "But bear in mind that Victoria remains our hostage for the next twenty-four hours."

Pained glances were exchanged by those gathered around.

"The man all of you saw here with the bag over his head is Reginald Clark, the notorious drug and prostitution prince and otherwise thorn in the side of Chicago. During the next twenty-four hours he will stand trial for his crimes. District Attorney Gordon is being given a second chance to do the job right this time. As is Juror Number Eight, Victoria Colby-Camp. The prince will be tried and sentenced and then that sentence will be carried out without delay. If any of you interfere in any way, including contacting the authorities, Victoria and Gordon will suffer the same sentence. Make no mistake," he reiterated, "we are watching and listening. One wrong move and Victoria dies first."

SLADE AND MIA helped Simon attend to the injuries, most of them minor, of the folks who had been held hostage. Ben Steele had returned with bad news—he, indeed, could not reach his target alone. He needed help. Ian had introduced him to Penny Alexander, a potential hire for the Colby Agency, who had just arrived. She wasn't scheduled to come on board for another week, but her special skills were needed now. If she was willing, so was the Colby Agency.

Before this day was over, Steele and Alexander had to attain their goal and stop this mockery of justice before anyone died.

Slade hoped like hell they could manage the feat. The internal workings of this state-of-the-art building were designed to prevent an intrusion. Now, the very design that had protected the agency and all others inside stood in the way of a rescue. By the time the two could reach the Colby offices, it might be too late.

Mia tapped Slade on the shoulder. He turned to face her. "We need to talk."

Slade glanced around the first floor of the coffee shop that would be closed this morning. The owner had graciously allowed the Colby Agency full use of the facility. The members of the Colby Agency were a bit damaged but they weren't beaten. There wasn't one of them who didn't want to do their part to end this nightmare.

Sadly, there was nothing anyone could do at this point except send in Alexander and Steele and hope that teamwork would succeed.

"I feel like I need to go to the new D.A." She bit her bottom lip. "Maybe he can devise a way to resolve this that doesn't alert those insane jerks. You know, bring aspects of the police in without the usual detectable communications."

Slade wasn't sure it would work but it couldn't hurt. He took Mia by the arm and located Ian and Simon, as well as Lucas. Jim's wife had arrived and was tending to his aggrieved soul.

Slade nodded for Mia to go ahead.

"The new D.A., Ashton Flannery," she began, "is a good man who believes in justice for all. I think maybe we can go to him. He would be the last person to just send the police in arbitrarily. He might be able to come up with a doable plan beneath the radar of those men."

The three men Slade knew had to agree considered her suggestion for a moment.

Ian spoke first. "You understand that your participation in this will be revealed in such a way that could expose you to prosecution if you go to Flannery."

Mia nodded. "I understand. It's the right thing to do. I don't care what I'm exposed to."

Slade felt a weak smile tug at his lips. He liked that she was so true and loyal to truth and justice. They might have gotten off on the wrong foot, but he knew her now.

"I can take her," Slade offered, "see

that the agency's interests are fully protected."

Jim shouldered his way into the huddle. "What's going on?"

Simon quickly explained what Mia had suggested. "This, of course, has nothing to do with Penny and Ben pursuing that avenue of infiltration. It's merely a backup plan," Simon clarified.

Jim considered the suggestion then turned to Mia. "If you believe you can trust this man, I'm on board. Anything we can do is better than standing here doing nothing."

That was a major step. Slade nearly swayed with the overwhelming relief.

"Jim and I," Ian offered, "will remain here to monitor the infiltration efforts." He looked to Lucas and Simon. "The two of you should get some rest."

"You know better than to suggest that I leave," Lucas retorted. "I'm not going anywhere until my wife is at my side."

"Jolie is on her way here," Simon interjected. "She had to get a sitter for the kids. I'll spend a few minutes with her and then I'm with the rest of you. I'm not leaving until Victoria is safely out of there."

"Go," Ian urged Slade and Mia. "The clock is running."

He didn't have to say the rest…. Time for Victoria was running out.

Chapter Nineteen

Flannery home, 7:50 a.m.

Slade parked the SUV he'd borrowed from Ian at the curb on the opposite side of the street from D.A. Flannery's house. "If he's up yet there are no signs of life."

Mia peered at the house across the street. Though it was almost daylight, it was still gloomy enough to have lights on inside. Flannery would be expected at work in another hour or so. He should be up. Maybe he was in the shower.

"He's widowed," she explained. "Lives alone. He could be taking a shower."

Slade nodded. "So we should just knock on the door."

They had agreed not to call since they couldn't be sure if their phone lines were being monitored. Slade had picked up on an uneasiness regarding the subject when he'd mentioned it to Mia. But she wasn't used to all the subterfuge.

"We'll knock on the door." Mia reached for her door and slid out of the SUV. Like Slade's truck, it was a lot higher off the ground than her little hybrid.

Slade came around the vehicle to stand beside her. "Quiet neighborhood."

"The school buses have run already. No kids at home to be noisy."

He nodded. "No outside dogs, either."

"One less worry," she muttered.

As they crossed the street, she couldn't help feeling a sense of doom settling onto her shoulders. Something wasn't right. Then again, maybe she just felt bad because she hadn't been completely honest with Slade about Flannery.

"You know," Slade said, leaning his head close to hers, "this feels wrong somehow."

"We must be on the same wavelength. I was just thinking the same thing." She kept the other part of her worries to herself.

As they approached the door, the intense oppression only heightened. Weird. Mia rapped on the door. Five seconds later, Slade reached around her and pressed the doorbell.

They waited.

Nothing.

Slade knocked this time. He pounded hard enough to wake the dead. She shivered. She'd had all the near-death experiences in the past twenty-four hours that she ever cared to have.

Another minute or two lapsed with no reaction.

"Let's go around back," Slade suggested.

Mia glanced at the house on the right and then the one on the left. No one appeared to be looking. So she followed him around to the gate at the side of the house. It wasn't locked, just a simple latch that let them through into the backyard.

The yard was lavishly landscaped. Even in the dead of winter it was breathtaking. More greenery than she would have expected. Lots of fancy rocks and pavers.

No lights in any of the windows at the back of the house, either, though. That was troubling.

"This is just weird." Mia liked this less and less.

"Time to put some of my less marketable skills to use." Slade winked at her.

She blushed then followed him to the

back door, which appeared to lead into a laundry room or mudroom. Putting her hands on either side of her face, she peered through the glass. Washer and dryer. Yep, laundry room.

He pulled out his wallet, removed a credit card and did the niftiest trick she'd ever seen. He slid it between the door and the frame and did some expert wiggling. The next thing she knew he opened the door as if he'd used a key.

"Wow. I'd say *less marketable*," she noted with a soft laugh. What else would she learn about this man?

Other than the very obvious facts that he was tall and gorgeous and kind and loyal and made her heart skip about every other beat. And that he was an amazing kisser.

Mia rolled her eyes. This was certainly not the time or place for such thoughts. Her reasons for breaking yet another law were serious…deadly.

They needed a break. Something had to give. Everything, including justice for her cousin, was riding on how this turned out.

"Mr. Flannery," she called out as they entered the kitchen.

This went on for several minutes. She alternately called his name and frowned when it became obvious that he had certainly been in the process of preparing for work. The shower was running in the master bath. Had been running for a few minutes. The mirrors over the two sinks were fogged. A suit was laid out on the bed.

Back downstairs his briefcase sat by the front door, next to the table where his keys and cell phone lay waiting for his exit.

"We've searched the entire house." Slade shook his head. "We have to be missing something."

Her gaze met his. "Basement?"

They moved back to the broad, sweeping stairs and opened the closet door built beneath. The closet was large, large enough to step into. On the far side was a door that led into the basement.

The moment they descended the first step, the smell of death assaulted Mia's nostrils. Her pulse sped up as did her feet.

Ashton Flannery lay sprawled on the basement floor. He wore white boxers and a white T-shirt. A single bullet hole in his forehead had leaked a significant amount of blood on the concrete floor.

Mia couldn't move. She stood there and stared. Trying to figure out if he'd killed himself…or…

No, no…that couldn't be.

Then she saw the note in his hand. Slade checked the man's carotid artery, shook his head, then tugged the note from his cold fingers. He stood, opened the neatly folded pages and stared at the typed note.

Mia and Slade,
I didn't want to make a mess upstairs. This is a warning. Don't get
any more bright ideas or the next
body you discover will be Victoria's.
Yours Truly: The MAN in charge.

Dear God! "How could they have
known?" Mia couldn't comprehend this.
It was crazy!

Slade turned to her, his expression
grave. "Did you talk to anyone else
before talking to me?"

Emotion lodged in her throat. "I…I
used the coffeehouse phone and
called…" She indicated the dead man
on the floor. "I didn't give him any
details. I just told him I needed to talk to
him right away. He—" she licked her
lips "—said I should come directly
here."

Slade closed his eyes. "Great."

Mia hung her head. "I'm sorry. I

thought it was okay since I didn't tell him anything." She touched Slade's arm. "I didn't mean to lie to you. I just had to be sure he would welcome our visit. I swear I didn't tell him anything."

"But," Slade countered, "you told *them* everything. Where you were going and who you were going to talk to."

Mia fell into his arms. Exhaustion was clawing at her. She was running on empty. She'd made a mistake. One that had cost a man his life. This was her fault.

Slade held her close, guided her up the stairs and out of the house. When he'd buckled her into the passenger seat of the SUV, he swiped at the tears on her cheeks. "We're going to get through this…together."

She nodded. "That's the only way."

There was no promise of tomorrow… only today…this moment.

It was time to stop planning for another day and start appreciating this one.

Slade closed her door and moved around the vehicle to slide behind the steering wheel. He started the engine and drove away.

Now they had another dilemma. Did they call the police and report the murder? As far as Mia was concerned, she was leaving that decision up to Ian, Lucas and Slade. She'd screwed up far too much already.

Slade braked for a traffic light. He glanced at her. "Ian and Lucas will know what to do."

The broken laws and accessory charges just kept piling up. But she could survive that… How could she live with being responsible for another human's murder?

How would they ever survive this mess?

She had just wanted justice for her cousin and all the others.

"Hey." He touched her cheek with the

tips of his fingers and turned her face to his. "Don't give up on me yet."

She laughed, though she felt no humor. "It's not you I'm giving up on. It's me." How could she have been so foolhardy? So utterly stupid?

"Does it matter that I'm not giving up on you?"

A smile prodded at her lips. "Yes. Yes, it does."

"Good."

He kissed her, softly, sweetly. She cherished this moment, this kiss. And the man.

No matter that everything else about her life was uncertain. He was the certainty she'd been looking for her whole life.

Chapter Twenty

Inside the Colby Agency, 8:05 a.m.

Victoria sat on one side of the long mahogany table in her conference room. Across the room Leonard Thorp stood next to his hired guns. Reginald Clark, the prince, remained bound in his chair, but the chair had been relocated to one end of the conference table. Gordon sat at the opposite end, sweat beaded on his forehead, his designer framed eyeglasses askew.

All seated at the table were scheduled to die before this day ended. Thorp and his men would never allow Victoria or Gordon to leave this building alive. Certainly Reginald Clark would not survive if this mock trial was allowed to play out.

Victoria thought of her husband, her son, and the many other family members and friends she loved. She also reflected on the many people her agency had helped, could still help.

A smile lifted the corners of her mouth. Her gaze settled on Thorp and his evil henchmen. She wasn't beaten. Nor was she finished…not by a long shot.

All she had to do was buy some precious time. The best of the best were waiting just across the street to do what had to be done.

And Victoria, well, she fully intended to do her part. This was not the end.

* * * * *

Rancher Ramsey Westmoreland's temporary cook is way too attractive for his liking.
Little does he know Chloe Burton came to his ranch with another agenda entirely....

That man across the street had to be, without a doubt, the most handsome man she'd ever seen.

Chloe Burton's pulse beat rhythmically as he stopped to talk to another man in front of a feed store. He was tall, dark and every inch of sexy—from his Stetson to the well-worn leather boots on his feet. And from the way his jeans and Western shirt fit his broad muscular shoulders, it was quite obvious he had everything it took to separate the men from the boys. The combination was enough to corrupt any woman's mind and had her weakening even from a distance. Her body felt flushed. It was hot. Unsettled.

Over the past year the only male who had gotten her time and attention had been the e-mail. That was simply pathetic, especially since now she was practically drooling simply at the sight of a man. Even his stance—both hands in his jeans pockets, legs braced apart, was a pose she would carry to her dreams.

And he was smiling, evidently enjoying the conversation being exchanged. He had dimples, incredibly sexy dimples in not one but both cheeks.

"What are you staring at, Clo?"

Chloe nearly jumped. She'd forgotten she had a lunch date. She glanced over the table at her best friend from college, Lucia Conyers.

"Take a look at that man across the street in the blue shirt, Lucia. Will he not be perfect for Denver's first issue of

Simply Irresistible or what?" Chloe asked with so much excitement she almost couldn't stand it.

She was the owner of *Simply Irresistible*, a magazine for today's up-and-coming woman. Their once-a-year Irresistible Man cover, which highlighted a man the magazine felt deserved the honor, had increased sales enough for Chloe to open a Denver office.

When Lucia didn't say anything but kept staring, Chloe's smile widened. "Well?"

Lucia glanced across the booth at her. "Since you asked, I'll tell you what I see. One of the Westmorelands—Ramsey Westmoreland. And yes, he'd be perfect for the cover, but he won't do it."

Chloe raised a brow. "He'd get paid for his services, of course."

Lucia laughed and shook her head. "Getting paid won't be the issue, Clo— Ramsey is one of the wealthiest sheep ranchers in this part of Colorado. But everyone knows what a private person he is. Trust me—he won't do it."

Chloe couldn't help but smile. The man was the epitome of what she was looking for in a magazine cover and she was determined that whatever it took, he would be it.

"Umm, I don't like that look on your face, Chloe. I've seen it before and know exactly what it means."

She watched as Ramsey Westmoreland entered the store with a swagger that made her almost breathless. She *would* be seeing him again.

Look for Silhouette Desire's
HOT WESTMORELAND NIGHTS
by Brenda Jackson,
available March 9 wherever books
are sold.

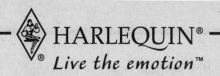

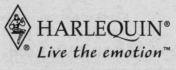

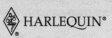

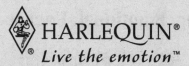

HARLEQUIN®
Super Romance®

...there's more to the story!

Superromance.
A *big* satisfying read about unforgettable
characters. Each month we offer *six* very different
stories that range from family drama to adventure
and mystery, from highly emotional stories to
romantic comedies—and much more! Stories
about people you'll believe in and care about.
Stories too compelling to put down....

Our authors are among today's *best* romance
writers. You'll find familiar names and talented
newcomers. Many of them are award winners—
and you'll see why!

If you want the biggest and best
in romance fiction, you'll get it
from Superromance!

Exciting, Emotional, Unexpected...

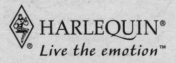

HARLEQUIN®
Live the emotion™

Harlequin® Historical
Historical Romantic Adventure!

*Imagine a time of chivalrous
knights and unconventional ladies,
roguish rakes and impetuous
heiresses, rugged cowboys
and spirited frontierswomen—
these rich and vivid tales will
capture your imagination!*

*Harlequin Historical . . .
they're too good to miss!*

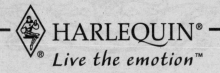